GEORGE'S MOTHER
and Other Weird Stories

Also by Susan Berliner

SOLDIER GIRL (Book Two of The Touchers)

AFTER THE BUBBLES (Book One of The Touchers)

THE SEA CRYSTAL AND OTHER WEIRD TALES

CORSONIA

THE DISAPPEARANCE

PEACHWOOD LAKE

DUST

GEORGE'S MOTHER
and Other Weird Stories

Susan Berliner

Published by SRB Books

ISBN: 978-0-9839401-9-7

Cover design by April Anderton
Layout by Rik of Wild Seas Formatting
Author's photo by Rachel Leib Photography

Published March, 2020

Printed in the United States of America

Praise for Susan Berliner's books:

The Sea Crystal and Other Weird Tales

"Once you start reading anything written by Ms. Berliner, you had better clear your calendar. Her characters are haunting, memorable, and real. It takes a special talent to be able to create a scene in a few pages, from beginning to end, and this is where the author excels. As soon as the story begins, you are thrust into a little microcosm where things look ordinary...mundane even. But then...plants start talking, or someone disappears, or someone who is there turns out that they were never even there in the first place!" — K.W. Skultety *Gimmethatbook*

"From chilling mirror images, to fairy tale lives, to a world of dark dreams that comes to life, there is so much to explore in Berliner's world...It was a lot of fun to try to figure out where the twist in each of these stories would be. Honestly, most of the time I was completely wrong about where I thought they were going. Which, of course, made it that much more fun!"
 — J. Nottingham, *Hopelessly Devoted Bibliophile*

"Around New Year's, my local cable station runs a marathon of Twilight Zone episodes...and that is sort of what this book put me in mind of - a little touch of the weird, but not too dangerous - something you could let kids read out loud during a sleepover. These stories are fun, and super-quick." — Rik Ty

After the Bubbles (Book One of The Touchers)

"I absolutely LOVED this book! I was sorry to get to the ending. Great ending, by the way. The story is so original. Lots of surprises. So suspenseful...Thankfully it's not a true story, but I kept thinking - what if." — Susan Zajicek

"I really enjoyed book 1! Very fun YA concept." — Eleanor Merry

"*After the Bubbles* is a great suspenseful story that holds the reader's interest throughout. I couldn't wait to see what would happen next." — Regina Munroe

Soldier Girl (Book Two of The Touchers)

"This highly anticipated second book of The Touchers series was, as usual, enthralling, un-put-down-able, and satisfying as hell. I urge all fans and devotees of the supernatural genre to read just one of her delightful and uniquely styled books, and promise, you, too, will become enthralled with her works."
 — Linda Commodore

"Just read *Soldier Girl* by Susan Berliner, the sequel to *After the Bubbles* and found it to be even better than the first. The tension permeates throughout the book. You never know when that shoe or toucher will drop...Ending was highly satisfying but sorry the story is over." — Lori Spinner

"Page turning novel...loved every second of it." — Andrew Ferrer

Corsonia

"Well written and well paced."   *– Julie's Book Review*

"I won't say *Corsonia* gave me nightmares, but my dreams were a bit more disturbing than usual! It was a great read, and gives the reader pause and makes you start thinking...could this actually happen? Not sure I ever want to find out!"
                                                        – Judy Barnes

"Thoroughly enjoyable vacation read! The author has an innovative way of weaving factual incidents or occurrences into fast paced fiction."   – Arlene Bender

The Disappearance

"I enjoy reading books with time travel - and this book took you back and forth constantly! It was done in such a way that had me almost believing it was really possible."   – Michele Bodenheimer, *Miki's Hope*

"There are many modes of time travel, but this one takes the cake - so different from others I've read!...This group of characters working together to bring down one culprit is so different, so eclectic; it's a wonder they ever met each other! But that's what makes it work! I love 'The Sting' all over again."   – Lila L. Pinord

"I just loved this book! This is one of those books that will call you to pick it back up if you have the self-control to set it down for a moment. I was pulled in throughout the entire story because I could not wait to see what would happen next."   – Dawn Fitzpatrick

Peachwood Lake

"It is a marvelous coming of age horror story."   *– Night Owl Reviews (Top Pick)*

"Where else are you going to find a fish horror story that brings a young girl's life into focus?...I have no trouble recommending this book for the pre-teen/YA horror lover. Five out of five fairy kisses for this reader."   – Dottie Taylor, *Tink's Place*

"Great read. Fun and suspenseful. Best fish story since *Jaws*!"   – Peggy Derevlany

Dust

"Susan Berliner gives us an amazing mysterious supernatural story in *Dust*. It intrigues and holds the readers' attention, while pulling them in and not letting them put it down."   *– Night Owl Reviews (Top Pick)*

"*Dust* picks you up and takes you on a whirlwind ride, pun intended, and doesn't let you go until the final climax...It's a great piece of escapist fiction and a book to easily get lost in."   – Patricia Lane

"Susan Berliner's first novel is filled with drama, laughter, and engaging characters...As a high school English teacher...I give *DUST* an A+!"   – Brittany Mott

Dedicated to the memory of Lisanne Harrington,

who loved to write stories and to read them—including mine.

Her insightful suggestions always improved my books.

"A short story, if it's a good story,

is like a child's kite—

a small wonder, a brief, bright moment."

— Sean O'Faolain

INTRODUCTION

Like my first collection of stories, these tales cover a wide variety of genres including thriller, horror, sci-fi, fantasy, and humor—all with a touch of the supernatural. However, unlike *The Sea Crystal and Other Weird Tales*, I couldn't arrange these stories in the order in which they were written because the genres would have been poorly mixed and the longest two—almost novellas—would have been close together. Now "The Imposters" leads off the book and "The Key" ends it.

As with *The Sea Crystal and Other Weird Tales*, some of these stories have interesting origins:

* "Megan's Crows" – Early morning caws disturbed a young child in my family. Our solution was simple: a noise machine. But that gave me an idea: What if the problem with the crows was much more sinister?

* "Hat Trick" – This is a sequel to "The Rapunzel Effect," a story in my first collection. I hinted that Deb would get into trouble with a sorcerer's hat—and of course, she does.

* "Skinny Alex" – A children's book editor who loved *The Sea Crystal and Other Weird Tales*, hired me to write stories for a major educational publisher. This girl-in-the-mirror concept was initially

approved for that project—until we discovered the program heads didn't want "self-image" themes.

* "507-9302" – Friends had a rogue house phone that made calls to neighbors by itself. The problem—a faulty connection—was soon repaired by their telephone company. In this story, the explanation for the calls is far more complex.

* "The Island" – I entered this tale in an online contest. The requirements: Write a horror story about a sole survivor trapped on a deserted island using 1,000 words or less—a challenge since my short stories are considerably longer. Although this tale wasn't a winner, I like it and hope you will too.

Happy reading!

STORIES

THE IMPOSTERS

"Time to get up, Denise."

Hearing that name jolted Dennie out of a deep sleep. "What did I do wrong?" she asked as her mother turned on the bedroom light.

"Nothing, sweetie."

"But you never call me Denise unless I've done something really bad—so what'd I do?" Dennie sat up, preparing for the worst, although she didn't remember her crime.

Her mother smiled as she stroked the girl's long black hair. "You've done nothing wrong at all, sweetie."

Dennie stared at her mother's placid face. Mom looked the same, down to the dimple in the left cheek. But her mother never played with her hair, her mother never called her "sweetie"—and her mother definitely didn't use her real name, which Dennie hated because it sounded like "the niece"—unless something was very wrong.

Denise, she called me Denise. Dennie looked into her mother's soft gray eyes. *Something is very wrong.*

———

After quickly dressing in jeans and a pink tee shirt, Dennie rushed to Greg's room and knocked on his door.

"Go away!" her eight-year-old brother ordered.

"It's important," Dennie whispered. "Let me in."

Greg opened the door just enough to stick out his tongue at her.

"Don't be such a baby," Dennie said, forcing herself inside the room and closing the door. "I've got to talk to you. There's something wrong with Mom. She's acting funny."

"What'd she do?"

"She called me 'Denise.'"

"So you did something bad. You screw up all the time."

"But she said I didn't do anything wrong. Then she called me 'sweetie' and played with my hair."

"Huh?"

"Yeah. Watch her at breakfast and you'll understand what I'm talking about."

"Denise! Where are you?"

"See?...Be right there!"

———

Dennie and Greg sat at the kitchen table spooning Cheerios while their mother stood at the counter closely watching them. "Do you want something else to eat, Denise?" Mom asked.

Dennie stiffened. "No, thanks."

"How about you, Gregory?"

The boy shook his head.

Their mother glanced at the wall clock and smiled. "Denise, it's almost time for your bus. Where's your backpack?"

"I don't use a backpack anymore. I just carry my books."

Mom smiled again. "That's right. I forgot." She turned to Dennie's brother. "Are you still using a backpack, Gregory?"

He nodded.

"Then go and get it."

"But my bus doesn't come till eight-thirty."

Mom continued to smile. "It's always a good idea to be ready early, Gregory."

Leaping out of the chair, the boy ran into his room, slamming the door.

"What's the matter with your brother?" Mom asked.

"I don't know," Dennie said, swallowing a last spoonful of cereal. "I've got to go now. Goodbye." Without looking at her mother, she scooped up her handbag and notebook and rushed outside.

———

After school, Dennie unlocked the front door and entered her house, nervous about what she planned to do. With no one home, she had a chance to investigate—maybe find some clue about what changed her mother into a weird-smiling stranger.

Tossing her bag and books on the hallway floor, she stepped into the kitchen and jumped.

"What's wrong, Denise?" Mom leaned against the counter, wearing an apron and munching an apple.

"Why are you home? Why aren't you at work?"

Mom gave her that big goofy smile again. "Oh, didn't I tell you? I quit my job because I've decided to be a stay-at-home mother."

"But you were so happy when you got that job. You said you always wanted to work for SuperTech—and they gave you a big raise last month."

Mom shrugged. "I changed my mind. I thought it'd be more important to stay here and look after you and Gregory."

"But when I started eighth grade, you told me I was big enough to be home by myself and watch Greg. You said..."

"Let's not argue, sweetie." Mom put her arm around Dennie's shoulder. "What snack would you like today? I baked brownies."

Dennie spotted the tray on top of the stove. "I don't like br...," she started to remind her mother, but then stopped. *What's the use? Do I tell her she doesn't like to bake?*

———

This time, Dennie didn't have to fight to speak to her brother. Immediately after she heard the school bus pull away, Greg came into her room.

"What's the matter with Mommy?" he asked, looking like he was about to cry.

Mommy? He hadn't called their mother that in years. "I don't know what's wrong, but I'll talk to Dad when he gets home and he'll find a way to make her better."

"She's so weird and scary—making brownies and smiling funny."

Dennie nodded.

"I want Mommy back."

"It'll be okay." Dennie got off the bed and hugged her brother, something she hadn't done in a long time. "We'll fix her."

Greg didn't say anything. He just stood there letting Dennie hug him and making soft sniffly sounds.

"It'll be okay," Dennie repeated, wishing she believed her own words.

———

Dennie ran to the front door as soon as she heard a key in the lock. She'd hidden in her room all afternoon, but was determined to be the first to greet her father.

"Hi, Denise. How's everything?"

Dennie recoiled as if she'd been slapped in the face.

"What's wrong?" Dad smiled, flashing the same phony grin as Mom.

"Nothing." Sprinting as fast as she could, Dennie dashed into her brother's room and shut the door.

Greg, lying on top of the covers, opened his eyes. "I heard Dad," he said. "Did you talk to him?"

"No."

"Why not? You promised."

Dennie sat on Greg's bed, trying to think of a good answer. "There's a problem," she began.

"Yeah, Mommy's weird."

"I mean with Dad."

"What's the matter with Dad?" Greg sat up and stared at his sister.

Dennie put her arms on his shoulders. "I'm sorry," she said. "Dad's weird too."

———

After a long moment, Greg spoke. "What're we gonna do?" he asked, his voice quivering.

"I don't know yet."

"Can we run away?"

"No. The police'll bring us back."

"Why? We can tell them something's wrong with Mommy and Dad."

Dennie shook her head. "It's not that simple. They still look like our parents so the police won't listen to us."

"Even if we say they're acting weird?"

"Greg, we can't just tell the police that our parents are calling us Denise and Gregory. Those are our names."

"What about the creepy smiles?"

"The police don't know the way Mom and Dad usually smile. They'll think we're the ones that're crazy, not them."

Greg lay down again and closed his eyes. "I want all this bad stuff to go away."

"We don't know that they're bad, just that they're different."

Greg opened his eyes. "You don't think they're bad?" he asked.

Dennie sighed. "I don't know, but I hope not."

"Denise and Gregory! Time for dinner!"

———

The Harrison family sat around the kitchen table, dining on fried chicken and mashed potatoes. Dennie played with her food, twirling potatoes on her fork and barely eating anything, although she loved fried chicken.

"What's wrong, Denise?" her mother asked.

"I'm not hungry."

"Would you like a sandwich instead?"

"No, thank you."

Mom never made fried chicken, claiming it wasn't healthy, and mashed potatoes weren't on her dinner menu either.

"The food is delicious, Beth," Dad said. "I'll have another drumstick, please."

Dennie frowned and sank lower in the chair. Her mother's name was Elizabeth and her father never called his wife, Beth. His nickname for her was Betty. Dennie glanced across the table at Greg, who hunched over his plate, looking as if he were going to cry.

She struck her leg out, trying to nuzzle her brother's foot. Greg lifted his head and stared at Dennie, who smiled, hoping that would help. But he lowered his head again and focused on the table.

Mom jumped up. "Guess what I made for dessert?" she asked.

"Brownies," Dennie muttered.

"No, something else." She walked to the counter, returned with a covered platter, and triumphantly lifted the lid. "Look at this!"

Dennie almost fell out of her chair. "You baked a chocolate cake?" she asked.

"I most certainly did."

"You never baked a cake before."

"Now that I'm home taking care of you and Gregory, I have plenty of time for cooking and baking."

"But you said we shouldn't eat cake because it's got too much sugar."

Mom laughed—a strange new cackle. "I said that? How silly of me. Now who wants a piece of this delicious cake?"

———

Dennie sat cross-legged on her bed trying to concentrate on math homework. Her parents weren't bothering her. Usually one of them demanded to see the assignment and then reviewed her work. *I guess that's a plus.* She shook her head. Checking homework meant they cared.

Tiptoeing out of her room, Dennie knocked softly on her brother's door. "Greg," she whispered when he didn't answer.

"Leave me alone."

"Are you okay?"

"No."

"Can I come in?"

"No."

Dennie opened the door slightly and peeked inside. Greg lay on top of the bed with his eyes closed. "Did you do your homework?"

"No."

"Greg, you have to do it."

"Why? Mom and Dad didn't make me."

"You still have to do homework."

"You're not my boss." He turned onto his stomach, covering his head with the pillow. "Go away."

"Greg, you have to do your work while we figure this out."

"But you said we can't tell the police."

"I've got an idea."

"Really?" Greg jumped up and faced Dennie.

"Yeah. I'm going to Mom's company tomorrow. Maybe I can find out why she quit."

"Can I come with you?"

"No. I'm going straight from school."

"You'll tell me everything?"

"Of course." Dennie gave her brother a big hug. "We're a team, Greg, you and me, and we'll figure this out together."

———

"I've got to stay after school today for a science project," Dennie told her mother the next morning.

"That's nice, Denise." Mom flashed that goofy smile and didn't ask for any details. "I'm baking a special treat today and it should be ready when you come home."

Dennie nodded before grabbing her sweater and running out of the house.

She had trouble focusing on schoolwork and must have acted funny because Gwen asked her if she was okay. She didn't want to tell anyone—even a good friend like Gwen—what was wrong so she said she was fine.

After school, Dennie took the bus to SuperTech Industries—just a ten-minute ride—another reason Mom had been so happy with her job. She entered the sleek five-story building, walked to the receptionist's desk, and asked to see her mother's boss, Mr. Fisher.

"Can I have your name please?" the red-haired lady with glasses said.

"Dennie Harrison. My mother worked here till yesterday."

The woman smiled. "So you're Elizabeth's daughter. Have a seat and I'll see if Mr. Fisher can speak to you."

Sitting in one of the chrome and black chairs, Dennie stared at the huge splatter paintings that covered the clean white walls. She didn't like the artwork, which seemed like the artist had just flung different colors on the canvas.

Frowning, she picked up her notebook and pencil and started doing math homework.

———

"You wanted to see me?"

Dennie raised her head and faced a broad-shouldered African-American man in a gray suit. "Do you know why my mother quit?" she blurted out.

"No."

"I thought she liked working here," Dennie said, standing.

"I thought so too."

"What happened?"

Mr. Fisher shrugged. "The day before yesterday, your mother suddenly announced she was leaving. When I asked why, she said she wanted to stay home, take care of you and your brother, cook, and clean."

Dennie nodded. "That's what she told me too. But I thought she loved being an engineer. And she was proud of the raise she just got."

Mr. Fisher shrugged again. "Her behavior puzzled me too. Please tell your mother that I'm sorry she left. SuperTech will miss her."

"Did something happen here?"

"What do you mean?"

"Did my mom's job change?"

Mr. Fisher paused before answering. "When she got the raise, your mom started a new project."

"What was it?"

"I'm sorry, but I can't divulge that information," Mr. Fisher said, shaking his head. "It's confidential." He smiled at Dennie. "Thanks for stopping in today. Your mother should be proud to have such a conscientious daughter."

———

"So what'd you find out?" Greg asked as soon as Dennie walked into the house.

"Shh." She smiled at her mother, who stood at the doorway of the kitchen, again wearing an apron. "Hi, Mom."

"Good afternoon, Denise. How did your science project turn out?"

"It was great." Giving her mother another beaming smile, Dennie headed for her room, followed closely by Greg.

"How about some gingersnap cookies? They're cooling on top of the stove."

"No, thank you."

Dennie leaped onto her bed and Greg sat next to her.

"So what'd they say?" he prodded.

"Her boss said he didn't know why she quit. But she started a new project at work and he wouldn't tell me what it was."

"You think that's what made her like this?"

Dennie shrugged. "Could be. It's some secret stuff that just happened."

"What about Dad? He doesn't work there."

"Maybe she infected him."

"How?"

Dennie shook her head. "I don't know yet."

———

As she finished eating a sloppy joe and french fries—another unhealthy dinner her mother had never allowed—Dennie studied her parents. If you didn't know them, on the outside they both looked the same. But they were so different.

Her father used to have a throaty laugh. Now it was a goofy hee-haw and he laughed at things that weren't funny, like what her mother was saying now.

"So when I made the cookies, I thought the recipe said 'sprinkle in the sugar,' but it really said 'add sprinkles with the sugar.'"

"Hee-haw!" Dad brayed, in his new donkey laugh. "The cookies taste delicious so the sprinkles weren't necessary." He munched on another gingersnap and smiled.

"Gregory, would you like a cookie?" Mom asked.

"No, thank you."

"How about you, sweetie?"

"I'm full." Dennie smiled and stood. "Can I be excused to finish my homework?" It was another lie. She had already completed her assignments.

"Of course," Dad said. "Beth, I'll be happy to eat all the cookies the children don't want." And then he laughed again. "Hee-haw!"

———

From her mother, Dennie knew a little about SuperTech Industries. The company specialized in robotics, inventing machines to make people's lives easier. It seemed like a good idea—a bunch of R2-D2s and Roombas sweeping floors and cooking—like obedient servants you didn't have to pay.

But now, as she fiddled with her iPad, Dennie wasn't so sure about the robot servant idea. She found SuperTech's website, clicked on the "Products" heading and scanned the listings. Nothing seemed suspicious—just a group of robot helpers doing household chores like cleaning floors and turning on lights. And the robots were all little metal machines that looked like Alexa.

Dennie returned to the home page and checked the headings again. When she saw "Ideas in the Making," she clicked. After glancing at the descriptions and pictures on the page, she grabbed the iPad and ran into Greg's room.

"I found something," she said, rushing to the bed where Greg lay on his stomach, playing a video game. "Here." Dennie placed the iPad on his pillow.

Her brother studied the human-looking machines on the screen. "You think Mom and Dad are robots?" he asked, his voice quivering.

"Maybe not robots, but robot-people." She pointed to the company's name. "Mom was working on a new project for SuperTech. Maybe she was part of the project—like a test subject."

"What about Dad?"

Dennie shrugged. "She could've done something to him, by accident or on purpose."

"So how do we fix them?"

"I'm not sure," Dennie said, squeezing Greg's shoulders. "But I'm going to find out."

———

Dennie only knew one of her mother's work friends—Aileen Clark. But she didn't have the woman's home or cell number and certainly didn't want to ask her mother.

What to do? Sitting on her bed, Dennie leaned against the wall and closed her eyes. A minute later, she had the answer: Aileen's work email had to be just like Mom's—eharrison@supertech.com.

She grabbed the iPad, entered aclark@supertech.com and typed: "Hi Aileen. Can you email me your phone number? I need to call you. It's important. Dennie Harrison. P.S. Don't call me or my mom."

After sending the message, she closed the iPad. There was nothing else to do until Aileen answered—and that probably wouldn't be until tomorrow when she went to work.

Unless she's like Mom. Dennie shook her head, trying to rid her brain of that scary thought.

———

As soon as Dennie came home from school, she checked her emails. There it was! *A message from Aileen.* Opening it, she read: "Hi Dennie. Call my cell, 863-7226. I hope everything is ok. Aileen."

Dennie grabbed her phone and punched in the number.

"Hello," Aileen said.

"Hi, it's Dennie."

"Are you all right? Your message worried me."

"I'm fine, but my Mom...Well, she's different, so I wanted to know if you saw something at work."

There was quiet on the other end.

"Are you there?" Dennie asked.

"I'm just thinking how to explain it," Aileen said.

"Explain what?"

"When Bill Fisher told us your mom quit, I went looking for her to find out why. Then I spoke to her and..."

"What'd she say?"

"It's not so much what she said, but her whole attitude was...a little strange."

"She told you that she wanted to stay home and bake cookies for me and Greg, right?"

"Yes."

"And she smiled funny?"

"Yes."

"Mom just started a new project. Were you working on it with her?"

"Yes."

"What's it about?" Dennie didn't mention that Mr. Fisher wouldn't tell her.

"Smarter robots, the kind that act like people."

"Aileen, my mom and dad, they're like robots—not like my parents. I think something must've happened to Mom at work. Greg and I are scared. Can you help?"

"Oh, honey, I'm so sorry...Did you tell anyone else about this? A friend? The police?"

"No, just you."

"Good. Are you home now?"

"Yes."

"Stay where you are. I'll be there in fifteen minutes."

———

Mom was baking her latest batch of cookies—or cooking dinner—Dennie didn't know exactly what was going on in the kitchen, but whatever it was, it was keeping her mother busy. She tiptoed to the front entrance, watching for Aileen.

Dennie opened the door before Aileen had a chance to knock. Then she put her left forefinger against her mouth and pointed to the kitchen with her right hand. Nodding, Aileen followed Dennie to her room, passing her mother, who was engrossed in a cookbook and didn't look up.

Dennie closed her door and leaned against it. "See?" she said.

"That's not my mom."

"She's different, but she's still your mother."

Dennie shrugged. "Only on the outside. That's why I didn't call the police. What happened to her?"

"I don't know for sure, but maybe..." Aileen stopped talking.

"Maybe what?"

"Maybe she decided to experiment on herself and your father."

"With the robot stuff?"

Aileen nodded.

"How could she do that?"

"Even though this program's designed for robots, there's a way it can be used on people."

"To turn them into robots?" Dennie asked.

"To alter their minds."

She stared at Aileen. "Then how do I get my parents back?"

"We have to find it."

"Find what?"

"The formula they're taking."

"Some kind of drug?"

"Yes, and both of them must be taking it daily."

"A pill?"

Aileen shook her head. "No, a liquid."

"Where should I look?"

"Start with your parents' bedroom or bathroom."

"Does this stuff have a name?"

Aileen shook her head. "It's just an experimental formula."

"What color is it?"

"The last version was a golden brown—kind of a honey color."

"Is it thick or thin?"

Aileen thought for a moment before answering. "More on the thin side."

Dennie stood. "If I find the drug and get it away from them, then my mom and dad should be okay, right?"

"I hope so," Aileen said, rising. "But nothing's definite since the formula's never been tested." She stared into Dennie's brown eyes. "Please don't tell anyone else about this, including the police. If

SuperTech finds out I told you about the Humanitoid Project, I'll be fired."

Dennie nodded. "I promise I won't say anything. I just want to get my parents back so I'll search the house until I find the drug."

"Good luck," Aileen said, kissing Dennie's cheek lightly. "Give a call to update me. Here's my number again." She scribbled on the back of a business card and handed it to Dennie, who studied the paper before tossing it on her desk.

———

"You have to keep Mom away from her bedroom so I can look for the stuff they're taking," Dennie ordered Greg after she briefed him on Aileen's visit.

"How?"

"Do something to stop her before she goes in." Dennie shrugged. "She may not even go there. She spends all her time in the kitchen anyway."

"But what if she wants to go inside? What do I do then?"

"Say you need help with your homework—or that something's stuck or broke." Dennie shrugged again.

"I'm scared," Greg said, his gray eyes watering.

"It'll be okay." She gave her brother a hug.

———

Dennie tiptoed into her parents' bedroom and quietly closed the door. She hadn't been inside since her mother and father had changed and as she studied the bedroom, she realized it had changed too. The room was much neater than she remembered.

She opened the walk-in closet door and all the shirts, pants, blouses, skirts, and dresses were neatly hung up. Nothing was on the floor or falling off a hanger. Even the sweaters piled on the top shelves were perfectly folded.

Dennie returned to the bedroom and marched to her mother's dresser, opening each drawer and checking the contents. Again, every item of clothing was neatly folded and the papers in Mom's messy junk drawer were clipped together and the pens were tied with a rubber band.

Her father's armoire was just as neat and so was the desk her parents shared. *No bottle of brown formula.*

The bathroom! Rushing into the attached room, Dennie flung open the medicine cabinet. She scanned the pill bottles, neatly aligned on the first shelf, and the various lotions and creams that filled the other two shelves.

One bottle was a honey brown color. She picked it up and read the label. "Cough medicine," she murmured, opening the container and smelling the contents. The liquid was thick, with the gooey sweet flavor she recognized. Sighing, Dennie returned the bottle to the shelf.

She opened the doors underneath the sink and examined the perfectly stacked piles of tissues, toilet paper, and bathroom cleansers. Frowning, Dennie backed out of the bedroom.

————

"Did you find the medicine?" Greg asked when Dennie returned to his room.

"No, and I looked everywhere." She hopped onto her brother's bed.

"I bet I know where it is," Greg said.

"Where?"

"In the kitchen—that's where she is all the time."

Dennie looked at him and nodded. "I think you're right. But if the stuff they're taking is in the kitchen, how can I find it without her seeing me?"

"Like you said, I can ask her to help with my homework."

Dennie shook her head. "No. She's always cooking something so even if she's in here helping you, she'd go back in the kitchen to check the food. I'll set my alarm and search tonight when everyone's sleeping."

"I'll help you look. I'm a good finder."

She grabbed Greg's shoulders. "I've got a better idea. You can be the lookout, watching to make sure Mom and Dad don't catch me searching the kitchen. That's an important job. I'll wake you when I'm ready to start."

15

———

When Dennie's alarm sounded at 2 a.m., she grabbed her flashlight and tiptoed into Greg's room. "I'm going to the kitchen now," she whispered, gently shaking his arms. "Stay awake and listen for them."

"Okay," her brother said, rubbing his eyes.

Pointing her flashlight on the floor, Dennie made her way to the kitchen. As quietly as possible, she opened each drawer and checked the contents—silverware, plastic bags and foil, can openers, paper towels. No brown liquid.

She switched to the lower cabinets—soaps and cleansers, pots and pans, canned goods. Again, no brown liquid.

She searched the upper cabinets, shining her flashlight on the plates, cups, and glasses. All the dishes were in neat piles. The pastas, grains, flour, sugar—everything looked normal.

Pancake syrups? They were brown. Maybe the drug was hidden with them. She opened each bottle and sniffed the contents. They were all thick and sweet-smelling.

Dennie eyed the top cabinets above the stove. They were too high for her to reach so, as quietly as possible, she lifted a chair and carried it to the range. Then, climbing onto the chair, she opened one of the upper cabinets.

"Denise, what are you doing?"

At the sound of her mother's voice, Dennie nearly fell off the chair. "My throat hurts so I'm looking for cough medicine." It was the first lie that entered her mind.

"Please come down."

Dennie stepped off the chair and faced her mother, who held a small bottle of brown liquid. "I have something that will make your throat feel better, sweetie," Mom said, smiling that creepy smile.

"No!" Dennie stepped backwards, leaning against the sink.

Her mother stood in front of her, blocking any escape. "Denise, don't be difficult. It tastes fine."

"Greg!" Dennie hollered.

"Please don't disturb Gregory."

"Greg! Get out!"

"Why should your brother get out, Denise? I know he's okay because Dad is with him." Still holding the bottle, Mom opened the cutlery drawer and lifted a spoon.

Dennie rammed her shoulder into her mother's arm, knocking the spoon on the floor. Then, without looking back, she raced through the kitchen and out the front door.

———

In the street, Dennie ran as fast as she could, which wasn't very fast since it was dark and she was cold, dressed only in a flimsy nightgown. She glanced at her shoeless feet. *At least, I'm wearing socks.* She'd figured padded feet would make less noise in her kitchen search.

When Dennie reached the end of her block, she switched to a quick jog and headed for the small shopping center less than a mile away. Although none of the stores would be open in the middle of the night, the center might provide a warm hiding place until morning when she could find help.

Greg was alone with them. That thought made her move faster.

She saw the line of buildings ahead, creepy-looking rectangular white boxes surrounded by blackness. She walked past the pizzeria, pharmacy, real estate office, and corner ice cream shop. Behind the storefronts, flanking the small parking lot, was an alcove filled with a dumpster and assorted junk.

Dennie found a discarded newspaper and a large smashed-in box. Wedging her body into the cardboard, she covered herself with pages of newspaper, closed her eyes, and huddled in the back of the recessed area.

———

"Squawk! Squawk! Squawk!"

The loud bird noises woke Dennie. Lifting her cramped arms, she wriggled her torso, surprised she had been able to sleep. The squawks were followed by pecking sounds as two large seagulls sifted through the dumpster for discarded goodies.

Dennie stood and stretched. It wasn't quite light yet and without a watch, she didn't know the exact time. Examining her nightclothes, she wondered how she could explain her appearance. "I won't," she muttered. Before losing her nerve, she walked past the line of stores to the intersection.

When the first car appeared, Dennie waved her arms, encouraging the driver to stop. But the stern-faced woman in the black SUV kept moving.

Dennie tried again with the next vehicle, a huge food truck. The man behind the wheel gave her a puzzled look, but didn't stop either.

As soon as she lowered her arms, a car pulled up to the curb. "Is something wrong?" a white-haired African-American man in a silver Honda asked as he opened the front passenger door.

"Yes," Dennie said. "I had a fight with my mom and ran away. Can you please call her to come get me?"

"Glad to hear you're ready to go home," the man said, picking up his phone. "You must be cold, dressed like that. What's the number?"

"It's 863-7226. Thanks."

The man punched in the digits.

"Hello," a woman's voice said.

"Your daughter is safe," the man began. "She's standing here in the street in her nightgown and no shoes, but wants to go home now."

Dennie reached into the car and snatched the phone. "Mom, I'm sorry I ran away last night when we argued about that syrup you wanted to give me." Dennie spoke quickly, not giving Aileen a chance to reply. "I'm at the corner of Starling Avenue and Gleason Road. Please get me."

———

"So your mother found you when you were searching for the formula," Aileen said as she drove Dennie to a nearby diner.

"Yes. That's why I'm dressed like this."

"I'm glad the kind man who called mentioned your clothing situation," Aileen said. "After I left a note for my family that I had to go to work early, I found a pair of jeans, a top, and flip-flops for you. They're a bit big, but better than nothing."

"What are we going to do?" Dennie asked. "I can't go home."

"During breakfast you can tell me everything that happened.

Then we're heading to SuperTech to talk to my boss." She smiled at the girl. "With his help, we'll figure out a way to get your parents back to normal."

———

"This has gone much too far," Aileen said as soon as she and Dennie entered Bill Fisher's corner office. "You've got to fix it."

He shut the door and returned to his chair before speaking. "Anything I do will ruin the project," he finally said.

Aileen grasped the desk with both hands, leaned forward, and stared at her boss. "Don't you understand? We're talking about people here—the Harrison family." She pointed at Dennie. "The girl escaped last night when Elizabeth tried to infect her and she thinks they've used the formula on her younger brother."

"I know they did," Dennie whispered.

"I'm sorry," Bill said to Dennie. "But I never told your mother to do this."

"No, you didn't tell her," Aileen agreed. "But you suggested to the team that it would be a good idea for someone to test the human formula to see if it worked."

"You can't prove I said that."

Aileen let go of the desk and backed away. "So that's your answer? You want to leave the Harrisons like this?"

"She'll run out of formula."

"Not for months—and you don't know how much damage it could do to their bodies by then."

"Please help us," Dennie said.

Bill Fisher shook his head. "I wish I could, but..."

"You can," Aileen interjected. "There's an antidote. It's another part of the project."

"But it hasn't been tested."

"Neither was the formula Elizabeth took. You've got to use the antidote on them. If you don't, I'm going to the police."

"And destroy the Humanitoid Project?"

"Screw the damn project!" Aileen took Dennie's hand and propelled the girl to the door. "You've got two hours," she said. "After that, I'm taking Dennie home and if her family isn't back to normal..."

"You'll be fired."

"Don't threaten me, Bill. You have till ten-thirty."

———

"Do you think Mr. Fisher will fix my parents?" Dennie asked when they sat in Aileen's car.

"I hope so, but I don't know."

"What are we going to do for the next two hours?"

Aileen turned to Dennie. "I'd like to see what's going on in your house. Are you up to it?"

"Dad probably went to work, but if my mom catches us..."

"We'll have to be careful so she doesn't see us. We can't get too close."

"All right," Dennie agreed.

———

Aileen parked diagonally across the street and they both studied the blue two-story house.

"It looks quiet," Aileen said.

"Do you think they let Greg go to school?"

"Probably. Otherwise, they'd have to explain why they kept him home."

"I don't see their cars," Dennie said. "But Mom's must be in the garage because I'm sure she's in the kitchen cooking something."

Aileen looked at the girl. "Your mother's not terrible like this, is she? She hasn't hurt you?"

Dennie shook her head. "No, but she's not my mother. She's a different person."

"And your dad?"

"Same thing with him, except he still goes to work. At home, he just does whatever my mom tells him to do."

"At least..."

Aileen stopped talking when a policeman tapped the window.

"What are you doing here?" the man, whose nametag read "V. Boraz," asked Aileen when she opened the door.

"Just sitting in the car and talking. Is that a crime, sir?"

The burly officer looked at Dennie. "Why isn't she in school?"

Aileen paused. "There was a situation..."

"Please step out of the car with your hands raised."

"But..."

"Do it now."

As Aileen stood face forward with her arms against the car, Officer Boraz turned to Dennie. "Is this woman your mother?"

"No."

"Why are you in the car with her?"

"I asked her to help me."

"And why do you need her help?"

Dennie didn't answer.

"Tell him," Aileen called.

"Yes," Officer Boraz said. "Get back in the car, show me your license, and then I'd like to hear the girl's story."

———

Dennie recounted what had happened to her parents. After she finished, the policeman shook his nearly-bald head.

"You don't believe me?" Dennie asked.

"It's too strange for anyone to make up, but..."

"Aileen works for SuperTech. She knows everything I said is true."

Officer Boraz, who had remained standing by the car window, looked at Aileen. "Did this stuff really happen?" he asked.

"Yes, sir. It did."

"And if we knock on the door of the girl's house, we'll find her mother...?"

"She's not my mother! She's like a robot!" Dennie leaned towards the policeman. "Please help me get that drug away from her."

The officer turned to Aileen. "What about that antidote the girl said your boss has?"

"I'm not sure he's going to use it because he doesn't want to jeopardize this project."

Officer Boraz opened the driver's door. "Both of you get out of the car and we'll see what's going on inside the house," he said. "I want to find out what a robot woman is like."

———

"Denise! We were so worried about you!" Elizabeth Harrison gave Dennie a big hug and kissed the girl's head several times. Then she smiled at Aileen and the policeman. "Thank you for bringing Denise home, Aileen, and you too, Officer."

"You're welcome," the policeman said. "But I'd like you to answer a question. Your daughter told me she ran out of your house in the middle of the night. Why didn't you call the police?"

Elizabeth hugged Dennie again. "She's such a smart and responsible girl. Her father and I knew she would come home."

"But she left in her night clothes—without shoes," Aileen pointed out. "If you were 'so worried,' why didn't you do anything?"

Instead of answering Aileen's question, Elizabeth simply smiled. "She's back home now, safe and sound, so everything is all right." Still smiling, she reached for Dennie, attempting to pull the girl into the house.

"I'd like to come inside too," Officer Boraz said. "I have a few more questions."

"Of course." Elizabeth opened the door, smiling even more broadly. "I have a spinach quiche in the oven. It will be ready soon and we can all enjoy a lovely brunch."

———

Sitting with Aileen and the policeman at the kitchen table, Dennie watched her mother cut four pieces of quiche. As she sliced, Mom continued to smile and make silly statements like, "What a beautiful day."

"Thank you," Officer Boraz said, taking a bite of the quiche. "This is delicious."

"Yes, it is," Aileen agreed. "But I don't remember you being interested in cooking."

"People change," Elizabeth said.

"I understand you quit your job earlier this week," the policeman said. "Any special reason why? Your daughter thought you loved working for SuperTech."

Elizabeth shrugged. "I decided it was time to do other things and as I told Denise, I wanted to be a full-time mother."

"I see," the policeman said, nodding. "And you decided you wanted to cook?"

"Oh, yes! It's wonderful." Her smile deepened, exposing the left cheek dimple. "It makes me so very happy."

Dennie pushed away her plate without eating anything and shook her head. She disliked spinach and her mother's response.

Officer Boraz stood. "I need to see the medications you're taking," he said to Elizabeth.

"Oh?" She gave the policeman a puzzled look. "Why?"

"Your daughter and your friend both think you're acting strangely."

Laughing, Elizabeth spread out her hands. "There's nothing wrong with me. I'm perfectly fine."

"Still, I want to see your medications."

Dennie's mother stopped smiling. "I don't have to show you anything. You need a warrant to search my house."

"Please, Elizabeth," Aileen said. "We're trying to help you."

"I don't need any help so, if we're all finished here, I've got a cake to bake." Smiling again, she reached for Aileen's chair.

"I'll be back with a search warrant," Officer Boraz said.

Elizabeth grabbed her daughter's wrist. "Thank you for bringing Denise back," she said.

"Aileen, help me!" Dennie shouted, trying to free herself.

"You can't leave her here!" Aileen told the policeman.

Officer Boraz extracted Dennie's fingers from her mother's grip. "I'm sorry, Mrs. Harrison," he said. "The girl's going into protective custody for now."

"But she's my daughter and I love her." Tears welled in Elizabeth's eyes. "You have no right to take her from me."

"Show me your medications."

She shook her head.

The officer quickly escorted Dennie out of the house.

Halfway out the door, Aileen turned around. "Elizabeth, please cooperate with the police," she said. "We're all trying to help you."

Dennie's mother slammed the door in her friend's face.

———

"What about my brother?" Dennie asked the policeman as they walked away from her house.

Officer Boraz didn't respond.

Dennie stood still. "They've given Greg that stuff. I'm sure of it. You can't let him stay with them."

The officer studied Dennie's face. "I can get in trouble for taking you away because there's no proof of drug use and your mother looked fine to me. So all of a sudden she likes to cook?" He shrugged. "No judge is going to consider that child abuse. I only took you out of your house because you were so frightened."

"But I'm more scared for Greg," Dennie said. "If they've turned him into a robot, I need to get him away from them. Even if they haven't..." She stared at the policeman. "Can you get permission to search the house?"

"I don't know."

"Then I'm out of here."

Officer Boraz grabbed Dennie's hand once more. "You can't keep running away."

"I'll live in the street if I have to! Anything's better than being with those robots that used to be my parents. And I'll figure out a way to save Greg."

As Dennie struggled to free herself from the policeman, Aileen caught up to them. "What are you doing?" she asked the girl.

"If he won't help me, I'm going to do this myself."

Aileen caressed Dennie's arm. "Honey, I'm still here for you and don't forget, I gave my boss an ultimatum."

Dennie stopped struggling and looked at Aileen. "Do you think he'll help?"

Aileen checked her wrist. "I don't know, but there's still forty-five minutes left."

———

Officer Boraz refused to leave. "I told her mother that she's in police custody so I'm responsible for the girl," he explained from the backseat of Aileen's car.

"But I'll make sure Dennie stays safe," Aileen said.

He shook his head. "That's not good enough."

"So you're just going to sit here with us?" Dennie asked.

"Yup. I've had lots of experience with sitting and waiting so I'm real good at it." He stretched his legs on the seat. "I'm going to rest a little. Let me know if your boss shows up."

———

"It's almost ten-thirty," Aileen said to Dennie as they continued to wait in the car.

"I guess Mr. Fisher's not..."

Aileen's cellphone rang. Reaching into her pocketbook, she grabbed the phone. "Bill, are you coming?" she asked.

Dennie heard Officer Boraz stir in the back seat.

As Aileen listened to her boss, Dennie strained to hear what the man was saying, but she couldn't make out his words.

"Then you've left me no choice," Aileen finally said as she returned the phone to her handbag.

"That didn't sound good," Dennie said.

"It wasn't."

"So your boss isn't going to do anything," Officer Boraz said.

Aileen nodded. "He said the antidote might not work and Elizabeth and Tom aren't in any real danger."

"That's a lie!" Dennie yelled. "They're robots!"

"But they're not hurting themselves or anyone else," Aileen said. "The formula just affects their personalities, making them act differently."

"Isn't that enough? My mom and dad are like make-believe people!" Dennie stared at Aileen wide-eyed. "You said you'd help me."

"I tried, Dennie, but Bill Fisher won't cooperate." She pointed to Officer Boraz. "And we told the police. He knows everything."

"What if they turned Greg into a freaking robot too?" Dennie turned to the policeman. "I have to get that stuff they're taking away from them. My brother's just a little kid."

"Like Mrs. Clark said, your mom isn't doing anything dangerous."

"She's not my mom!" Dennie shouted as she opened the door and raced out of the car.

———

Dennie had no idea where to go. She just knew she had to get away—from Aileen, from the policeman, and especially from her robot mother. *Greg...* She needed to find out if they did anything to him. *School?* They wouldn't let her sign him out. *His bus...*

Dennie kept running—not easy in Aileen's flip-flops—until she reached the small shopping center where she had hidden the previous night. Now the stores were open, with several cars parked in the adjoining lot.

Dennie headed to the back alcove and reconstructed her cardboard bed, bending the large box so she could fit into it. Then she crawled inside and closed her eyes, hoping to think of a solution.

———

When Dennie opened her eyes, her legs and arms felt stiff like she'd fallen asleep. After standing and stretching, she peeked out of the enclosure. *No police cars.* When she'd told Officer Boraz her story, she hadn't mentioned where she'd spent the night. And she hadn't told Aileen either.

She walked around the corner to the ice cream shop and looked through the window at the wall clock. It was just after two so she still had time. Greg's bus would be home in about an hour.

A woman and little girl exited the store laughing and licking vanilla ice cream cones. As Dennie stepped out of their path, she realized she was really hungry. But she had no money.

She scanned the row of stores. In front of the pizza place, an outside table had something on it. Dennie hurried there and scooped up a discarded slice, minus only a couple bites. After gobbling the pizza, she hurried back to the alcove.

———

Dennie hid behind the leafy tree across the street from her house, waiting for Greg's bus. She didn't see a police car or anything else unusual. *Nobody cares...*

Wiping the thought from her mind, she stood motionlessly, watching the road. A few minutes later, she heard the rumble of an arriving bus. After the driver released the stop sign and flashed his red lights, Greg stepped down.

"Over here," Dennie said, speaking in a loud whisper.

Greg turned to his sister's voice and looked at her.

"Here," she repeated.

Crossing the street, Greg approached the tree.

"Are you okay?" Dennie asked.

"Why wouldn't I be okay?"

"Mom and Dad."

"What about them?"

"Did they make you swallow that syrup they're taking?"

"Just a little bit. It tasted real good."

"Greg, that drug turns people into robots."

"But I'm not a robot. See?" He stuck out his tongue at her.

Dennie studied him carefully. "No, you're not. I wonder why."

"Are you coming back home? I tried to help last night, but Dad came into my room. I was scared at first, but after the syrup, I felt better. Maybe you should try some."

"Never!" Dennie stared at her brother. "You're not scared of Mom and Dad anymore?"

"No. They're nice to me. Mom even gave me a bunch of candy."

"Greg! They're not real people!"

He shrugged. "I don't care. I like them better 'cause they don't yell or make me do things. I'm gonna go inside now. I bet Mom's baked a cake or cookies..."

"Greg! Don't go in there!"

Her brother ran to the house.

———

Dennie slumped against the tree and closed her eyes, trying not to cry. *Everything was wrong...*

"I knew you'd be back."

When she opened her eyes, Dennie saw Officer Boraz's grinning face.

"Are you ready to go home now?"

"Please don't make me."

"I watched you talk to your brother just now and I know you were worried about him. Is he okay?"

"He's not like my parents, but he's different."

"In what way?"

"He's not afraid of them anymore."

"That's a good thing."

Dennie shook her head. "No, it's not. They made him take some of that robot formula and now he likes them—he even likes my Mom's cakes."

"The quiche was delicious."

"But that's not my mother! She doesn't cook and bake. She's an engineer."

The officer put his arm around Dennie's shoulder. "People change, but they're still your parents, and they love you."

Officer Boraz held Dennie's hand firmly as they crossed the street together.

———

SUPERTECH INDUSTRIES BOASTS THE WORLD'S SMARTEST ROBOT!
by Scott Earlman

Is Data, the *Star Trek* android, a reality?

According to SuperTech Industries, a leading manufacturer of robotic products, the answer is a resounding, "Yes!"

"We have succeeded in designing a robot that looks, thinks, and acts just like a human being," William Fisher, head of the company's Humanitoid Project, told reporters Thursday at a news conference at SuperTech's Central Street headquarters.

"Unlike Alexa and other virtual assistants, the Humanitoid robot has feelings and emotions," Fisher said as he introduced "Felicia," who is capable of performing a large variety of household tasks.

After the plastic-encased life-sized girl robot answered basic questions about herself in a pleasant monotone (she enjoys cooking and washing dishes), she proceeded to dust and vacuum a mock living room.

"I'm sorry I don't have enough time to bake a fresh batch of cookies for you," Felicia said. "But I made some before you came." Then she handed out chocolate chip cookies to everyone present. [Reporter's note: The cookies were great.]

At the end of the presentation, Fisher thanked the SuperTech employees who participated in the Humanitoid Project, singling out former engineer, Elizabeth Harrison. "We couldn't have succeeded without her help," he said.

When asked why Harrison was no longer with the company, Fisher explained she had left to be a full-time mother. "Like Felicia, Elizabeth discovered she enjoys baking cookies," he said.

DO OVER

Kenny sat in his wheelchair holding the old photograph. He had found the picture at the bottom of his desk drawer earlier in the day and couldn't stop thinking about it.

In the photo, he stood in front of his apartment building wearing a tight tee shirt and shorts, clothes that showed off his buffed physique—the kind of pose an eighteen-year-old would make when everything in life was great. And it was.

Tank had taken the picture with his Polaroid camera and afterwards the two of them watched the photo develop. Kenny remembered how cool it had been to see his image slowly form on the white glossy paper—like some kind of magic trick.

It was the last photo of him standing, the last picture before the accident.

How long had it been? Kenny shook his head in disbelief. *Fifty-three years this summer.* Closing his eyes, he tried unsuccessfully to stop the tears.

———

Kenny heard the street sounds even before he opened his eyes. And when he did, he saw the zooming cars and laughing kids. Somehow he was outside, in front of his apartment building. And even crazier, he was young and strong—and standing. He stared at his perfect legs, dumbfounded.

"What'cha lookin' at?"

That voice! Kenny lifted his head and there he was: Tank, the muscular giant who had been his best friend those many years ago.

"Come check out the picture." Tank waved his Polaroid camera at Kenny.

Then, just like he remembered, the two of them watched the photo develop—the same photo Kenny had been holding seconds ago.

"What's today's date?" Kenny asked.

Tank gave him a friendly shove. "You're kiddin', right? You know it's July nineteenth—and tonight's the big night."

*July 19th...*The night of the accident, the night Kenny would lose the use of his legs and Tank, his best buddy, would lose his life.

———

Tank was talking, but Kenny was no longer listening. "What's wrong?" Tank asked.

Kenny smiled. "Nothing at all. I was just thinking."

"Happy thoughts about tonight, I bet?' Tank grabbed Kenny around the shoulders, hugging him playfully. "That show's gonna be fantastico!"

*The Megitones...*They had tickets for the rock and roll concert, but never made it there. The accident happened on the way.

"I don't think we should go," Kenny said.

"Is this another joke?"

Kenny shook his head. "No. I heard the show's not supposed to be good because the lead singer..." He stopped talking when he couldn't remember the guy's name.

"Johnny Cantallano?"

"Yeah. I heard he's got laryngitis."

"Nah. You heard wrong. They would've cancelled if Johnny was sick. Tonight's gonna be super. I'm goin' home to eat and shower and I'll pick you up at seven, bud."

———

*Maybe...*Kenny leaned against the brick facade of the apartment building, formulating a plan.

The accident happened at 7:18. He knew the exact time from the police report. That's when the twelve-wheeler swerved into Tank's Mustang, the truck driver trying to avoid hitting a drunk's car that shot out in front of him.

Nobody wore seatbelts back then, although the Mustang had been so mangled that it probably wouldn't have made a difference. Tank died instantly and it took the police and medics over an hour to free Kenny, whose legs were crushed in the wreckage.

I know what to do. Kenny smiled at his simple, but brilliant, idea.

———

"What took you so long?" Tank asked Kenny as his friend settled into the front passenger seat of the red Mustang. "I don't want to be late for the concert."

"Sorry...I had a stomachache. Must've been something I ate today." Although that wasn't true, dinner had been a surreal experience for Kenny—sharing a meal with his long-dead parents. His mother had been puzzled when Kenny hugged her and burst into tears. *Eighteen again, walking, parents—Everything was crazy.*

"You okay now?"

"Fine." Kenny shook himself out of his reverie and snuck a peek at his watch, set to the correct current time: 7:25.

"Now I gotta drive real fast." Tank stepped on the gas and the Mustang surged forward.

"No! Just drive normal speed. We'll be okay."

Tank shook his head. "I don't know about that. You're makin' me take local streets instead of the highway so the trip's even longer."

"I told you, I just heard on the radio—right before you picked me up—there's a bad accident on the Cross-Bronx. You don't want to get stuck in that."

"I guess."

"We'll get to the concert on time. I bet they won't even start singing till after eight."

"I hope."

"You'll see."

―――――

Kenny was right. The Megitones didn't walk onstage until eight-fifteen and by then, he and Tank were in their seats. Not surprisingly, Johnny Cantallano's voice was fine and the concert was super.

As the two of them left the theater, Kenny couldn't believe his good fortune. Tank was still alive and he was walking next to him. *What now? Do I get to live my life over on two good legs?*

"You okay, pal?"

"Yeah, Tank. I'm fine."

"You sure? You're so quiet now and you were real quiet in there. Usually you holler and whistle."

Really? Kenny had no memory of his pre-accident concert demeanor. "Sorry," he said. "I've just been thinking about stuff."

"We should be able to use the Cross-Bronx going back," Tank said as he unlocked the car. "They had plenty of time to clear that crash."

"Take the long way, just in case," Kenny said. "We don't know how bad it was." *Or maybe there was no accident because the Mustang wasn't on the expressway.*

"And besides, we're in no rush to get home," he added.

"True." Tank jabbed Kenny's arm lightly as he drove out of the parking lot. "Great time tonight, buddo."

―――――

Kenny lay in his childhood bed in his old room—the one in his very-much-alive parents' fourth-floor apartment—unable to fall asleep. He lifted his legs under the sheet. *Still working.* And Tank was home in his bed, alive and well. *Did I change everything?*

When Kenny woke up the next morning, he was still in the apartment and it was July 20th—just a typical lazy summer Saturday—not the day after the accident, the first day of his lengthy hospital ordeal. Next door, he could hear his mother singing softly along with a big-band song on the radio as she cooked breakfast.

Kenny dressed and ambled into the small kitchen.

"How was the concert?" his mother asked, smiling as she flipped the pancakes.

"Great!"

"No trouble driving there and back?"

"No trouble at all...Where's Dad?" His father, a bakery goods deliveryman, didn't work on Saturdays.

"Frank called in sick so your dad had to do his route, but he'll be home by one...Sit down and eat. You must be hungry."

Just like Kenny remembered, his mother's pancakes were terrific.

––––––

Kenny's father wasn't home at one o'clock and he didn't call either. Even in those pre-cellphone days, it was easy to find a telephone. Booths were all over the city and phones were in every store his father delivered to.

By three o'clock, Kenny's mother was pacing the living room and Kenny, although just as nervous, was trying to reassure her. "Don't worry," Kenny said. "Dad's okay."

"Then why isn't he calling?"

"Maybe the truck broke down and he can't get to a phone."

"You know he treats that truck like it's his baby, Kenny, so it's always in wonderful condition. He's never even gotten a flat tire."

"He could have driven over a nail—something that wasn't his fault."

Kenny was still trying to come up with positive possibilities when the phone rang. His mother ran into the kitchen and Kenny heard silence while she listened to the caller.

"I'll be right there," she whispered, hanging up the receiver.

When she returned to the living room, Kenny's mother's face was pale and her eyes were moist. "There's been an accident," she said. "Dad's in Jacobi Hospital."

––––––

Kenny and his mother walked until they hailed a taxi and neither spoke during the ten-minute ride. At the hospital, his mother explained the situation to the receptionist, who directed them to the emergency room. When they got there, they were told Kenny's father was in surgery.

They sat in the operating room's visitors' lounge, waiting for word from the doctor. Kenny looked at his mother, who turned away from him, crying silent tears. Although he wanted to console her, Kenny couldn't think of anything comforting to say so he remained quiet, thinking his own gloomy thoughts.

Two hours later a surgeon entered, still in his operating scrubs. "Mrs. Antelluci?" he said, quietly.

Nodding, Kenny's mother stood and walked slowly to face the doctor. Kenny joined her, tightly grasping her hand.

"We did all we could," the surgeon began.

"Is my husband going to be all right?" his mother asked, her voice barely audible.

"He's going to live."

"Thank goodness!" She squeezed Kenny's hand.

"But it was a bad accident and he had serious damage..."

"What kind of serious damage?" Kenny interrupted.

The doctor hesitated, shaking his head sadly. "His legs were crushed. I'm sorry, but he won't be able to walk."

———

Won't be able to walk...won't be able to walk...won't be able to walk...

Like a recording, the doctor's awful words continued to play over and over inside Kenny's head. But when he opened his eyes, he realized he was no longer in the hospital with his mother and the surgeon. He was in his own apartment again, holding the old photograph in his wrinkled hands.

Glancing down, Kenny discovered he wasn't sitting in a wheelchair. He was in the kitchen, seated on a regular chair. Touching his legs gingerly, he flexed them, stood, and took a few steps. The legs worked fine.

I can walk, but... Kenny looked around his apartment. What was different? Except for the missing wheelchair and other accommodations for his paralysis, everything looked the same. Even with a lifetime of mobility, nothing had changed.

Using his healthy legs, Kenny rushed to the bedroom. Clutching the iPad, he quickly googled his father's name: Salvatore Antelluci.

The accident—the one they had been discussing in the hospital moments ago—was mentioned in the obituary. The doctor had been right. His father never walked again and died twelve years later, fifteen years before his original death.

Tank? Kenny googled his friend's name: Raymond Sautek. Tank hadn't died in a car accident. However, the following year he had been drafted into the army and sent to Vietnam, where he received a Purple Heart: Tank died in the battle of Khe Sanh.

Kenny closed the iPad and sobbed.

MEGAN'S CROWS

"Mommy! Mommy!"

Her daughter's cries immediately woke Callie Rowland and sent her running to the room next door. "What's wrong, honey?" she asked.

Megan sat up in bed and hugged her mother. "The crows, Mommy. I'm scared of the crows."

"I know they're loud, but they're just birds." Looking at the digital clock on the shelf, Callie saw it was 4:44 in the morning. "You've got to go back to sleep," she said, gently lowering the child and tucking her under the blanket.

"No." The little girl bounced up, shaking her head.

Callie rubbed her daughter's shoulders and tried another approach. "Megan, even though crows are big birds, you're much bigger than they are. The crows are scared of you."

"No, Mommy. They're not."

"Honey, please," Callie begged. "The birds live outside. They're nice birds and they don't want to hurt you."

Megan again shook her head. "Not these birds," she said. "These birds want to hurt people."

"Oh, honey." Callie held the girl tightly. "You know birds don't want to hurt us so why did you say that?"

With tears streaming down her cheeks, Megan stared at her mother. "Because the birds told me," she whispered.

———

When Megan didn't mention the crows again during the day, Callie figured the early morning episode was a one-time thing. Her daughter seemed perfectly fine, painting and dressing her dolls in the morning and playing on the backyard slide and swing in the afternoon.

At one point, a crow flew overhead, squawking a loud "caw." Callie tensed, but Megan ignored the noise so Callie said nothing, not wanting to reintroduce the thorny subject.

During dinner, Megan ate macaroni and cheese and jabbered steadily about Cookie Monster and Ernie. "I want a rubber ducky like Ernie has," she said.

"For your birthday, honey." That was Callie's standard comment for all the "I wants."

"And I want more Cookie Monsters."

"For your birthday."

Life with a four-year-old. But Callie wasn't complaining. Even though the marriage didn't work—Nolan was a good-for-nothing lazy bum—she adored her sweet little girl. Fortunately, Callie was able to support Megan with her web design work, all done from their cozy new house. Yes, she was isolated here. But soon she'd make friends and find playmates for Megan.

———

"Mommy, I'm scared! Mommy, come here!"

Jumping out of bed, Callie raced into Megan's room and turned on the light. "Honey?"

"The crows, Mommy!" The hysterical little girl flung herself into her mother's arms.

"Megan, we talked about the crows yesterday and I thought you understood they're nice birds that won't hurt anyone."

"No! They're bad birds that want to hurt people!" She hugged her mother tightly.

Callie looked at Megan's clock. The dial read 4:51. "Honey, that's silly and it's much too early to wake up. You shouldn't be afraid every time you hear a loud crow."

She wiped her daughter's tears with a tissue. "When we were outside yesterday, we heard a crow and you weren't scared."

"That wasn't a bad bird."

Holding her daughter away from her, Callie stared directly into the girl's blue eyes. "What do you mean?"

"That was a good crow. These ones are bad."

"How do you know the difference?"

"The bad crows talk to me."

Callie hugged her daughter tightly and smoothed the girl's brown hair. "Honey, crows don't talk to people."

Megan, a serious look on her teary-eyed face, nodded her head up and down. "Yes, they do, Mommy. The crows talk to me when I'm sleeping and their bad words wake me up."

———

After a lengthy negotiation, Callie finally convinced Megan to go back to sleep. As part of the deal, she agreed to stay with the girl until morning. She also agreed to hold hands.

"You won't let go, Mommy," Megan had said, clutching Callie's fingers. "Promise."

So Callie had promised.

The crows were quiet now and Megan was sleeping, a deep normal slumber. But Callie couldn't sleep. She had a serious problem and wasn't sure how to deal with it. Her daughter was convinced that crows—not all, but some—talked to her, telling her bad things.

Callie sighed. She had never encountered a situation like this with Megan. The little girl was fine otherwise. *What to do?*

She rolled over in the little space next to her sleeping daughter, trying to get comfortable while still holding Megan's hand. *I'll call Dr. Valencia tomorrow.*

———

In the morning, Megan acted like nothing had happened. Callie wasn't thrilled about bringing up the subject of the birds, but felt it was necessary. "Do you remember the crows waking you up?" she asked during breakfast.

"Yes, Mommy," Megan said, sipping her milk.

"But you're not scared now?"

The girl shook her head. "The bad birds are gone."

"But they'll come back?"

"Not in the day. Just at night."

"You're sure about this?"

"Yes." Megan, a serious look on her face, nodded several times. "They told me."

"The crows told you?"

Megan nodded again. "They're very bad birds, Mommy. But they're sleeping now. They'll wake up later..." She started crying. "Mommy, I don't want them to talk to me! Make them stop!"

Callie rushed over to hug her daughter. "I'll stop them, honey," she said. "I'll make sure the bad birds won't bother you."

———

After Callie put on an Elmo video for Megan, she called Dr. Valencia's office and asked the pediatrician to recommend a therapist. "As soon as possible, please," she added. "Megan's been having terrible nightmares."

"Oh, I'm so sorry," the sympathetic receptionist said. "What kind of nightmares?"

"About crows. She hears them early in the morning."

"I think that's pretty common for little kids."

"But Megan thinks the birds talk to her and she's terrified."

"I'll speak to the doctor as soon as she's through with her patient," the woman promised.

Ten minutes later, the receptionist called back with a name: Dr. Samuel Lundquist. Callie immediately phoned Dr. Lundquist's office, and after explaining the urgency, was squeezed into his afternoon schedule.

———

Dr. Samuel Lundquist's waiting room was bright and colorful, boasting large windows, peach walls, and an alphabet rug topped with yellow and green toy-filled bins. Megan found a caped and helmeted Grover doll and while they waited, flew him around the room, proclaiming, "I'm Super Grover!" in a squeaky pretend voice.

"Miss Rowland?"

Callie looked up from her magazine and faced a smiling man— younger and better-looking than she had pictured. "Yes." She returned his smile. "And this is Megan."

The therapist knelt when he reached the girl, who had stopped flying Grover to stare at him. "Are you giving Grover a ride?" he asked.

Megan nodded seriously.

"I love flying Grover too," he said, holding out his hand. "May I have a turn?"

Megan deposited Grover in the therapist's palm and he raced around the room with the doll, shouting, "Watch out! It's Super Grover!" in a passable imitation of the character's high-pitched voice.

Megan giggled and Callie put her arms around her daughter as they watched the man's antics. After a few minutes, he returned Grover to Megan. "That was fun," he said, still smiling. "Now how about we all go inside and talk a little?"

———

Dr. Lundquist—or Dr. Sam—as he asked Megan to call him, listened to Callie's recounting of Megan's fear of the bad crows. After she finished, he turned to the girl. "Is that what happened?" he asked.

Megan nodded seriously.

"Is there anything else about the bad crows that I should know?"

The little girl shook her head.

"Are you sure?" Sam prodded. "Or will telling me make the crows mad?"

Megan started to shake her head again, but then hesitated. "They don't like me talking about them," she whispered.

"Did they say they would hurt you if you told people what they say?" Sam asked.

Megan nodded solemnly.

"Okay." Sam sprang up from the windowsill, where he had been sitting. "Then we won't talk about the bad crows anymore. Tell me about your favorite toys. What things do you like to do?"

For the rest of the session, he didn't say another word about the crows. "I'll call you tonight to discuss my thoughts on what's going on here," Sam said to Callie as she and Megan left the office.

———

"Your daughter's a lovely little girl," Sam began. "But she's got a vivid imagination."

"I know," Callie agreed.

"She's convinced those birds are talking directly to her—and she's transferred all her fears into the crows, making them the embodiment of evil."

"But why just certain crows? She's not afraid of all the birds, just the ones in the early morning."

"I don't know," Sam admitted. "But that doesn't matter. What's important is she's really scared and we need to make her feel safe."

"How?"

The therapist was quiet for a moment. "Let's try the simplest solution first," he said. "Tomorrow, buy one of those white-noise machines and set it loud enough so she won't wake up and hear the crows. If she doesn't hear them, they can't talk to her. Right?"

"I hope so," Callie said.

———

"Mommy! They're coming!"

Callie pulled off the blanket and raced into her daughter's room. However, Megan wasn't in her bed. Standing in the semi-darkness, Callie squinted, but still didn't see the little girl. "Megan, honey, where are you?" she asked.

"I'm over here."

Following the whispery voice, Callie opened the closet door and found her daughter cowering under the hanging clothes. Kneeling, she hugged the shaking girl. "Oh, honey."

"They're coming," Megan repeated, tears streaking her cheeks.

"What's coming?" Callie asked, although she already knew the answer.

"The crows. They said they're going to hurt me, and you, and everybody." The girl burst into tears. "Mommy, I don't want to stay here. I want us to go somewhere far away."

"Honey, don't be scared," Callie said. "I spoke to Dr. Sam last night and he told me how we can stop the crows from talking to you."

"How?" Megan looked at her mother, her eyes widening.

"We're going to get a machine that makes a loud noise—like wind or rain—and you won't hear the crows so they won't be able to talk to you."

Megan shook her head. "I'll still hear them."

"I don't think so," Callie said. "The noise will be too loud. We'll buy the machine today and turn it on tonight." She gave Megan another hug. "Now let's go back to bed. You can sleep in my room until it's time to get up."

———

Callie made sure Megan was involved in choosing the noise machine. She had the salesman turn on several models until the girl found one she liked.

Actually, Megan didn't have a preference for a specific sound. She didn't care if the noise was wind or rain or a waterfall. "How loud can you make it go?" she asked the man.

Callie purchased the machine with the highest volume and placed it on Megan's top shelf. "You should sleep well tonight, honey," she said, kissing her daughter and turning on the device. "Good night!" The white noise was so loud that she had to shout her words.

———

"Mommy! Mommy! Come here!"

Megan's shrieks drowned out the blaring of the new machine. When Callie switched on the light in her daughter's room, she saw the girl sitting up in bed and crying hysterically.

"They don't like that noise!" Megan shouted, pointing to her top shelf. "Turn it off!"

Callie pressed a button and the noise stopped, except for Megan's sniffling. Sitting on the bed, she hugged her daughter.

"It made them so mad," the girl whispered. "The crows said they have to talk to me—to tell me what they're going to do."

'Honey, they're not going to do anything."

"Yes, they are and it's gonna be very bad."

"Honey, they're just birds."

The girl shook her head. "They're not. They're monsters and they're coming for us."

"Do you know when they're coming?"

"No," Megan said. "But they told me it'll be soon."

———

"It didn't work," Callie informed Sam. She had left a message for the therapist after breakfast and he phoned twenty minutes later, apologizing for the delay in returning her call.

"Here's my cell number so you can get through immediately," Sam said, rattling off the digits. "And don't worry, we'll find another way to alleviate Megan's fear."

"But she's so terrified of those crows and she's really convinced they're talking to her."

There was a short pause before the therapist spoke. "Can Megan sleep with you in your bed tonight? It might make her feel safer till we solve this."

"Of course she can, if you think it will help."

Sam made a soft chuckling sound. "I'm not sure and I haven't helped you yet. I'll try to come up with another way to resolve Megan's problem and call you this evening. Meanwhile, hang in there. We'll figure this out."

"I hope so," Callie said. But she didn't feel very hopeful.

———

"Here's my idea," Sam said when Callie picked up the phone. "Set your alarm a little before the time Megan's been waking up and snuggle tightly. This way, when she hears the crows, you'll be right there with her."

"How will that help?"

"I'm thinking that she feels alone and vulnerable, which is why she created this bad-crow scenario in the first place." He paused before speaking again. "Maybe someone in her life deserted her. I don't want to pry, but you've never mentioned a husband."

It was Callie's turn to be silent. "He hasn't been in the picture since Megan was an infant," she finally said. "My daughter doesn't even ask about him. You think she made up this scary crow stuff because she misses her father?"

"I don't know, but it's possible."

"Should I bring up the subject?"

"You can prod gently and find out if it's bothering her. But first see what happens tomorrow morning when the crows come. Maybe you being close will stop her from hearing them."

"I'll try it."

"Call me tomorrow morning on my cell and let me know if it helped."

After hanging up the phone, Callie walked into her bedroom, kissed her sleeping daughter, and set the alarm for 4:30 am.

———

When the alarm sounded, Callie quickly shut it off so the noise wouldn't wake Megan, who slept peacefully on the other side of the bed. She inched closer and wrapped her arms around the sleeping child. Then she waited.

"Caw! Caw! Caw!"

Callie tensed when she heard the birds, but her daughter continued to sleep. *Maybe?* Callie continued to hold Megan tightly and closed her eyes.

"Mommy!"

Callie, her arms still cradling Megan, instantly awoke. "I'm here, honey," she said, caressing the girl. "You're safe with me."

"No. The crows don't like me with you. They want me in my bed."

"They told you that?"

The girl nodded somberly.

"Are they talking to you now because I don't hear them?"

"Nobody but me hears them. They just talk to me."

Although Callie continued to hold and caress Megan, she felt the

47

girl shivering under the blanket. "It's okay, honey. Really."

Megan grasped Callie's arm. "No, it's not okay. They're here."

"They're not here, honey."

Megan stared at her mother. It was nearly dawn and in the semi-darkness Callie could see the fear in the girl's eyes. "Look out the window, Mommy."

Callie stepped out of bed and lifted the edge of the curtain. Across the street, in the empty lot, were crows—perhaps a hundred big black birds. She couldn't count them all. None of the crows moved or cawed. They just stood there as if they were waiting for something.

Callie's fingers trembled as she let go of the curtain and returned to bed. "What are the birds going to do?" she asked, hoping her voice sounded normal.

"They're going to hurt us," Megan whispered.

———

"It's Callie Rowland," she told Sam when he answered his cellphone. "I'm sorry to call so early, but I didn't know what else to do."

"What's wrong?" the sleepy voice on the other end asked.

"Megan wasn't imagining the crows. They're real. Right now, at least a hundred of them are outside our house."

"What!"

"And Megan says the birds are going to hurt us."

"Did you call the police?"

"I wanted to, but Megan got hysterical and wouldn't let me. She's sure that will make the birds really mad."

"Give me your address and I'll be right over."

After she gave Sam the information, Callie peeked out the window again. The crows still filled the lot across the street—and it seemed like there were even more big black birds—all facing the house, none of them moving or cawing. *A black-feathered army.* Callie shivered at the creepy sight.

Trying to compose herself, she returned to the bed and sat near Megan. Her daughter's eyes were closed, but the girl wasn't sleeping.

"Honey, Dr. Sam's coming to help us," Callie said, stroking Megan's shoulders.

The girl shook her head. "He can't help us."

"Sure he can." Callie said. "He's a very smart man."

Pulling the blanket over her head, Megan started to cry.

———

When she heard the approaching car, Callie raced downstairs and opened the door for Sam. "I'm so glad you're here," she said.

"This is surreal—all those silent crows."

"Did the birds do anything when you got out of the car?"

The therapist shook his head. "They didn't react at all."

"Megan is terrified and I am too."

"Where is she?"

"Still in my bed."

"I'd like to talk to her."

"Of course." Callie led the man upstairs to her bedroom. "Honey," she whispered. "Dr. Sam is here."

Megan wrapped herself deeper in the blanket and didn't open her eyes.

"Let me help you," the therapist said, leaning over the girl.

"No." Megan shook her head.

Callie heard a loud noise outside. When she opened the curtain, all the birds were ruffling their feathers as if preparing for flight. "The crows are mov...," she started to say before the cawing forced her to stop.

The shrieking noise was so deafening that Callie put her hands over her ears and watched as, like synchronized flyers, the crows arranged themselves low in the sky and formed a circle around the house. The cawing stopped, but the birds continued to fly past the windows.

"They're only a couple feet away," Callie whispered to Sam.

Megan hadn't moved. She was still enveloped in the blanket with her eyes closed.

"Megan," Sam said. "You have to work with me."

"No," the girl whispered.

The loud cawing started again. When Callie looked out the window, the circling birds seemed closer. She heard footsteps on the roof, followed by clumping sounds. "The crows!" she shouted. "They're on the house!"

Callie looked outside again and there were no birds in the sky.

———

The cawing stopped. In its place were constant thumping sounds as the birds pecked and clawed at the roof and siding. Then Callie heard pinging noises as several birds threw themselves against the bedroom windows.

"Megan," Sam said quietly. "You have to end this."

"I can't." The girl, her eyes still closed, shook her head.

"Make the birds stop."

Callie stared at Sam. "What are you saying?" she asked.

"It's Megan. She's controlling the birds."

"That's impossible."

The thumping sounds continued.

Another bird flung itself against the window, creating a large crack. The next bird crashed into the same window, enlarging the opening. Callie heard glass breaking downstairs.

"Megan!" Sam ordered. "Make the birds stop!"

"I don't know how!" the girl said, tears falling from her closed eyes.

"You can do it. Tell them to go away."

There was a fluttering noise as two crows flew into the bedroom and landed on the dresser.

"Shoo," Callie said, waving at them, but the birds ignored her and didn't move.

Another three birds flew into the room and then more and more until about twenty crows covered the room, perched on the dresser, night tables, windowsills, and bed. The birds stood motionless.

Callie moved closer to Sam and Megan. "What are they waiting for?" she whispered.

"I don't know," Sam said.

One crow began flying around the room and others followed

until all the crows flew in a circle near the ceiling. Then a bird landed on Callie's shoulder. "Get off!" she ordered, trying to dislodge the bird. But it didn't move.

"They won't listen to you," Sam said. Two crows landed on his head.

Callie heard the fluttering of wings and watched more birds fly into the room until crows occupied every inch. "I can't move," Callie whispered as some birds covered her head while others perched on her arms and feet.

"I'll try again," Sam said. "Megan, all the crows are in this room, right here. Tell them to leave the house—now!"

"I can't," the girl said, shaking her head and sobbing. She pushed the cover higher, temporarily dislodging five of the birds.

One of the crows on Callie's head bit her scalp. "Ow!" she shouted. "It's pecking me!"

"Me too!" Sam said. "Megan! Stop this! The birds are hurting us!"

"No!" Callie yelled as another crow attacked her bare foot, drawing blood. She looked at the therapist whose arms were dotted with red marks.

A bird reached down and pecked Callie's forehead. She swiped at the crow, but missed as blood trickled down her cheek. "Megan, please!" she begged.

The girl sat up and opened her eyes, glancing around the room with a look of bewilderment and horror. Then she closed her eyes tightly.

There was a loud fluttering noise and Callie watched the birds fly out of the room. She rushed to the window in time to see the flock of crows stream out of a downstairs window and into the brightening sky.

The house was silent.

———

"They're all gone," Callie whispered. She turned to her daughter, whose eyes remained open. "What happened, honey?" she asked.

"The bad crows went home," the girl said quietly.

"Are they coming back?" Callie asked, rubbing her sore head and gathering tissues to absorb the blood on her face, arms, and foot.

"No, they're not," Sam said. "Right, Megan?"

Megan nodded seriously. "They don't want to talk to me any more."

Callie handed Sam a bunch of tissues. "Is it over?" she asked.

He took the tissues and shrugged. "The crows, yes, but I don't know about other creatures." Dabbing the bloody marks on his arms and cheeks, Sam faced Megan, who still sat in bed, staring straight ahead. "Is anything else talking to you?" he asked.

There was a buzzing noise and a fly entered the bedroom, landing on the girl's head.

"Just him," Megan said.

HAT TRICK

I held the long cylindrical hat in my hands and examined it. The hat was bright red, decorated with little black stars, diamonds, and other shapes. A sorcerer's hat, I was sure.

How did I know? Because I discovered the hat in my great-aunt Jessie's bedroom closet and she'd been a witch.

"Hey, Marla!" I called as I twirled the hat. "Look what I found!"

My roommate came to the door, glanced at the hat, and groaned.

"Don't worry," I assured her. "I'm not going to do anything."

"You didn't think you did anything last time either," she pointed out.

In December, when we'd moved into this cottage that Aunt Jessie left me in her will, I found a book of spells and stupidly said a few Latin words—just four—and then my hair wouldn't stop growing.

"I'm only putting the hat on my head for a moment to see how I look. I promise I won't say a word."

"You shouldn't even do that," Marla advised.

But I didn't listen to her. Placing the sorcerer's hat on my head, I climbed down the stepladder, walked to the mirror above the dresser, and smiled at my reflection.

"Take it off, lady wizard, before something bad happens," Marla warned.

"Sure." I removed the hat.

"Now put it back where you found it."

"I'll do that too." And I did.

"See," I said, when I returned. "Nothing bad happened."

———

Ten minutes later, I was still reorganizing boxes on the top shelf of the closet when the doorbell rang. *Now? Saturday morning?* We weren't expecting visitors.

"Marla, please get the door!" I yelled.

"I'm in the bathroom!"

After racing down the stairs, I peeked through the slit and saw Wally smiling at me. "Why're you here?" I asked when I opened the door.

"That's some greeting, Deb," he said, stepping inside.

"You could've called first or at least texted." I'd met Wally in freshman English Comp and dated him a couple times. But now we were just friends—and hardly that. He could be a pain.

"I really need to talk to you and wanted to do it in person."

This didn't sound good. "About what?"

"Well..."

"Come on, Wally. What did you do—and how am I involved?"

"Can I at least sit down?"

I indicated one of Aunt Jessie's overstuffed living room chairs and Wally sat while I stood in front of him.

"You're making me nervous," he said.

"That's only because you've got something to be nervous about. What's going on? Has it got something to do with those damn rocks?" We were in the same Introduction to Geology class this semester.

"Kind of."

"Spit it out, Wally. Now." I crossed my arms and waited.

"Okay...I signed you up for a field trip in Crestview this afternoon. I'm sorry, but they needed one more person or Professor Larson was going to cancel so..."

"Wally, you're a real rat!" I shouted. "How could you...?" But I stopped yelling when I heard a big poof sound in the chair where Wally was sitting, followed by a cloud of white smoke. And when the smoke cleared, Wally was gone. In his place in the chair was a giant gray rat.

———

I stared at the rat and the rat stared at me. Then it lifted its two front legs and squeaked.

"Wally?" I whispered.

The rat bobbed its furry head and squeaked again.

"Marla!" I shouted. "Come down here!"

"What's going on?" she asked as she entered the living room.

I pointed to the chair.

"That's a rat!" Marla shrieked, running behind me and clutching my shoulders. "Get it out of here!"

"Umm," I mumbled. "It's not really a rat."

"Yes, it is! A great big one! Get it out of the house or call somebody!"

"It's Wally," I whispered.

"Wally's a guy. That's a rat. I know the differ..." Marla stopped talking, came out of her hiding place, and studied my face. "Deb, what did you do?"

"I didn't do anything, really I didn't. I just got mad at Wally, called him a rat, and then this happened." I nodded towards Wally the rat, who sat quietly in the chair studying us.

"That sorcerer's hat. You had it on your head before he came here."

I nodded. "I guess the effects must have lasted."

"I warned you not to wear that thing."

"And I should've listened to you, but it's too late now. Maybe I can call Wally a person and bring him back that way." I knelt so I was closer to the rat. "You are Wally the college student, not a rat," I commanded.

No poof, no cloud of smoke, no Wally. The rat stared at me with its beady eyes and squeaked.

———

I shook my head. "I'm sorry, Wally," I said. "Really, I am. When I called you a rat, I didn't mean it."

He tilted his furry gray head and snarled.

"What do I do now?" I asked Marla.

"I don't know."

"Maybe..." Running into the bedroom, I climbed up the stepladder and grabbed the sorcerer's hat from the corner of the closet.

"Don't tell me you're putting that dangerous magic thing on your head again," Marla said.

"It can't hurt."

"Yes, it can. You can make things worse. Please, Deb, don't even try it."

"I have to." Wearing Aunt Jessie's hat for the second time, I faced Wally the rat. "You are Wally, the human being," I said, slowly and clearly. "You are not a rat."

I waited for the poof and cloud of smoke. But neither happened and the big rat continued to occupy the upholstered chair. Removing the sorcerer's hat, I stashed it on the closet shelf again.

———

When I returned to the living room, Marla was kneeling next to the chair with the rat. "Do you see what's happening?" she asked, pointing to Wally.

"See what?"

"The rat's bigger."

And it was. When Wally first became a rat, he'd filled about half the chair's cushion. Now he covered nearly the entire seat. "Do you think I did that too?" I asked.

Marla nodded. "It's the hat. Promise me you won't ever wear it again."

"Okay, I promise. But we've got to do something to get Wally back."

"What about the witch?" Marla asked. "That strange lady who helped you when your hair wouldn't stop growing."

"Lucinda something?"

"Yes."

"That's a good idea," I agreed. "Let's go there right now. I just have to get the magic hat."

"Shouldn't we call first?"

"No," I said. "She might tell us not to come. And if she's not in her store, we know where she lives." I turned to Wally. "Are you ready for a road trip?"

―――――

Marla remembered the store's name—Magically Yours—and checked the address on her phone. It was in Londondale, a forty-five minute ride, but we didn't have a choice. Wally the rat was still growing. When he got off the chair and trotted to the car (We weren't picking him up!), he was about two feet long.

As I drove, Marla searched for the witch's full name. "They're called Wiccans now," she reminded me. "But I can't find any Wiccan named 'Lucinda.'"

All of a sudden, I remembered. "It's Rosinda, not Lucinda. Try that."

"Got it!" Marla shouted. "Rosinda Farquand."

"I just hope Rosinda knows how to turn Wally back into a person."

There was a series of loud squeaks from the back seat.

"I know, Wally," I said. "I'm really sorry about all this."

―――――

We reached the row of small shops that included Magically Yours and I parked the car. As Marla opened the back door for Wally, I carefully removed the bag with Aunt Jessie's hat from the trunk.

I heard squeaking and saw the rat, now nearly three feet long, standing on its hind legs. "Yes, Wally," I said. "We're going to fix your situation now."

Magically Yours was open so Marla and I walked in quickly, with Wally behind us. Rosinda, sitting at the rear of her cramped dark little shop, looked up from the book she'd been reading. "What have we here?" she asked, standing.

"Do you remember me?" I asked. "It was in late December and

57

you helped..."

"The hair!" she said, shrieking and pointing to my head. "You're the girl with the hair to the floor! I still laugh about that."

I never thought the experience was so funny, but I smiled at the blonde witch. "And I really appreciate how you ended that spell. But now I've got another big problem."

"Oh?" She gave Marla and me a puzzled look. "What's wrong?"

I stepped to the side so she could see Wally. "This is," I said.

"What the hell!" Rosinda shouted, moving backwards until her body pressed against a bookshelf. "Get the big rat outta here!"

"It's not really a rat," I explained. "That's Wally and he's a guy."

"Sure looks like a rat to me!" The witch inched away from us along the rear wall.

"Well, you see..." I began, removing the sorcerer's hat from the plastic bag.

Rosinda stopped moving and pointed to the red hat. "Where'd you get that?" she asked.

"I found it in Aunt Jessie's closet."

"Don't tell me you put it on your head."

I nodded.

The witch shook her head and sighed. "Didn't I warn you how dangerous it is to use magic?" She glanced at Wally, who'd been standing quietly behind us. "Couldn't you have done the usual thing and turned him into a frog? You had to pick a rat?"

"It was an accident," Marla whispered. "She didn't mean to do it."

Rosinda walked up to Wally, bent down, and stared at him. "Is he growing?" she asked. "He looks bigger than just a minute ago."

"I put on the hat a second time to try to turn him back into a person," I whispered.

"You're a goddamn idiot!" Rosinda yelled. "That hat is super-sensitive. Give it to me!"

I handed her the sorcerer's hat.

———

"What do we do now?" I asked quietly.

"You do nothing," Rosinda said, holding the hat far away from her body as she walked. "You've done enough already." When she reached the counter, the witch lowered the hat gently to the floor.

"But look at poor Wally," I said, pointing to the gigantic rat, now over four feet tall. "He can't keep growing like this. You've got to change him back before people miss him. It's as if he's vanished."

There was a loud poof sound and a cloud of white smoke engulfed Wally. When the smoke cleared, the big rat was gone.

"What happened?" Marla asked, staring the emptiness beside her. "Where's Wally?"

Rosinda glared at me. "Didn't I just warn you not to do anything?"

"But..."

"That meant do nothing—including opening your big mouth."

"I'm sorry," I whispered.

"Like I told you, that's a real powerful hat—not meant for anyone's head except a sorcerer or witch."

"Well, you're a witch," I said.

"Yeah, I am," Rosinda agreed. "But since the hat was on your head twice today, you've still got its powers and I can't wear it yet."

"Where'd Wally go?" Marla asked again.

Rosinda shrugged. "Who knows? He could be anywhere."

"Is he still a rat?" I asked.

"I don't know the answer to that one either," the witch said.

This conversation was not inspiring me with great confidence. "So how do we get Wally back?" I asked.

"We can't do anything until tomorrow," Rosinda said. "Maybe by then, any magic left over from you wearing the hat will be gone."

———

Early next morning, Marla and I drove back to Londondale. Although Magically Yours wasn't open on Sundays, Rosinda had agreed to come to the store to help us. Ignoring the "Closed" sign, Marla knocked on the door and Rosinda let us in.

"Thanks, so much," I said, smiling at the blonde witch.

"Don't thank me yet. I haven't done anything."

"But you will," I continued, still smiling. "I know you'll be able to bring Wally back."

Rosinda grunted. "Glad you're so sure."

"Is there a problem?" Marla asked.

"Yeah, there's a big problem."

"Oh?" This didn't sound good.

"I've been reading up on these hat spells," the witch said, indicating the counter where three large books lay open. "And I'm not sure I can fix what you did."

"Can't you just put on the hat and say that Wally's a person?"

Rosinda shook her head. "It's not so simple."

"Should I put on the hat and say something?"

"No!" Rosinda and Marla shouted in unison.

———

I stood silently, afraid to open my mouth.

"Is there some way we can help you?" Marla finally asked.

"I don't know." Sitting on a stool behind the counter, the witch flipped the pages of one of the big books. "They all say to do different things."

"Maybe we should try them all," I suggested.

"No!"

Maybe I should keep quiet.

"What things do they say to do?" Marla asked.

"One says mix eye of newt with vinegar and Tabasco sauce, another says spin the hat while singing and dancing, and the third book..."

She stopped talking and shook her head.

This time I kept quiet. By now I knew she didn't want my input. Marla didn't say anything either and we both waited for Rosinda.

"This book," the witch began, lifting one of the heavy volumes. "It says I gotta go outside to an open field, build a fire, fill a big pot with water and red rose petals, and put it on the fire. Then, when the water boils, I gotta wear the hat and ask for your friend's return."

"The first two sound easier," I whispered.

"Really?" Rosinda stared at me. "I'm fresh outta eye of newt."

"How about singing and dancing with the spinning hat?" Marla asked.

"I didn't tell you everything about that one," Rosinda admitted.

"There's more?" I asked.

"Yeah. You gotta spin the hat while naked in an orange grove."

"All right, then," I said. "Where's the nearest open field?"

———

According to Rosinda, there was a small park a few blocks away. But first we needed red rose petals. "Is there a flower shop around here?" I asked.

Rosinda shrugged. "Yeah, Londondale Florist. But it's closed Sundays."

"And I guess you don't have any red roses on hand," I continued.

"You guessed right."

"Maybe we can get some petals from a rose bush," Marla suggested. "They're in bloom now."

"We drive around town and go on someone's lawn?" I asked.

"The book didn't say the petals had to be fresh, did it?" Marla asked Rosinda.

"No."

"So couldn't we use petals that fell off the roses?" she continued.

"I dunno if old petals will work," Rosinda said, shaking her head. "Sometimes these spell books leave out important stuff."

"Then we'll have to take a live rose from somebody's garden," I said. "We need to get Wally back."

———

After Rosinda went to her apartment to get matches and fill a large pot with water, we drove through Londondale, the witch directing us to streets with the biggest yards. We saw zillions of bushes—many with flowers—but no red roses.

"Doesn't anybody here like red roses?" I asked.

"Make the next left," Rosinda instructed. As soon as I turned, Marla shrieked. "Red roses! Stop right here!"

I parked the car in front of a huge Colonial with a lush weed-free lawn and perfectly trimmed matching bushes on both sides, including two with dark red roses. "Everything here's so neat, they'll probably notice a missing flower," I said.

"I'll do it," Marla offered. "No one will see." She rushed to the nearest rose bush and pulled off one flower. As she raced to the car and stepped inside, the front door of the house opened and a middle-aged man appeared.

I drove away before he could do or say anything. I don't think taking a rose off a bush is a crime, but it would've been tough explaining why we did it.

———

"Is it legal to build a fire here?" I asked Rosinda when we reached the nearby park.

"You wanna get a permit?" She placed the pot on the grass in an empty area near the car and gave us an order: "Go find sticks."

Marla and I collected twigs and small branches, which Rosinda arranged in a circle. Then she lit a match and as we watched, the flames shot up and she placed her pot on top of the sticks. "Gimme the rose," she said.

After Marla handed Rosinda the flower, the witch tore off the petals and tossed them into the pot. When the water boiled, Rosinda put on Aunt Jessie's sorcerer's hat. "What's your friend's name again?" she asked.

"Wally," I said.

Rosinda nodded, closed her eyes, and waved her arms over the pot. "Oh, great magic hat," she chanted. "Bring Wally here to us."

There was a loud poof, followed by a cloud of white smoke. When the haze cleared, the rat was back.

———

"What the hell just happened?" I shouted.

Rosinda shrugged. "Sometimes these spell fixers don't work exactly right."

"'Exactly right?' He's still a rat!" And it was the giant-rat version of Wally, now nearly as tall as me. He raised his two front legs and squeaked happily. At least he was glad to see us.

"Lemme try again," Rosinda said. "Gimme your friend's whole name and age."

"Wally Levitt and I think he's nineteen," I said.

"Twenty," Marla corrected. "His birthday was last month."

"Oh, great magic hat," the witch said, moving closer to the boiling pot. "Thank you for returning Wally. But we want the original Wally Levitt, the twenty-year-old male human being."

I waited for the poof and cloud of smoke, but nothing happened. "What's wrong?" I asked.

Rosinda pointed to the boiling pot and the fire. "I think this set-up's only good for one spell fix."

"You mean we have to do it all again?" I stared at her in disbelief.

"Yeah."

"New everything—fire, water, red rose petals?"

The witch nodded.

"To the car," I said, turning around.

"Wait a minute," Marla said. "First we have to put out the fire. And what about him?" She pointed to Wally. "I'm not riding in a car with a huge rat. I know it's Wally, but still..."

"Doesn't matter," I said. "He's too big to fit."

After we emptied the water on the fire, dumped the petals, and waited for the pot to cool, Marla drove the witch to get new water and rose petals. I was left in the park with Wally, who was still growing.

———

People hadn't bothered us when we made the fire, but now I was out in the open, standing next to an enormous rat. I looked for a hiding place and spied a leafy tree. "Come on," I said to Wally, pointing to the oak. "We're going over there."

But as we rushed to the tree, a boy on a bike spotted us. I heard him call his friends and a minute later, three curious teen bikers surrounded us.

"What's that?" the tall skinny kid asked. "Some kinda giant rat?"

"Yeah," I agreed. "It's a rodent from South America." I knew some large rat species lived there.

"What's it doing in Briarwood Park?" the pudgy teen asked. "That's gotta be against the law."

"No," I lied. "It's all legal. We have a special permit for Wally."

"Cool." The long-haired kid with glasses whipped out his phone and snapped a photo. "It doesn't bite?"

"Oh, no," I said, caressing Wally's soft fur. "Wally's very tame. Do you guys want to pet him?"

"Nah," the tall kid said, taking a step back. "That's okay."

And then the boys on the bikes were gone.

———

As we sat under the tree waiting for Marla and Rosinda, I apologized to Wally again for getting him into this mess. "I'm so sorry," I said. "I know it's been hard for you."

"Squeak!" the rat whimpered, stretching its now six-foot-long body on the grass.

"This'll be over soon. When they come back, Rosinda will turn you into a guy again."

"Squeak!" Wally's rat-voice was louder and sounded much sadder.

"I feel real bad about all this...It was so dumb."

"Squeak! Squeak! Squeak!"

I stopped talking and the two of us waited silently.

———

"Deb, where are you?"

When I heard Marla's voice, I jumped up, waved my arms, and shouted, "Over here!"

Marla ran towards me, but stopped when she saw Wally. "He's grown even more," she whispered.

"Where's Rosinda?"

"She's in the parking lot with all the stuff. We have to get sticks for the fire again."

I pointed to the giant rat. "What about Wally?"

"Leave him here till we're ready so maybe no one'll notice him."

"Some kids already did." I faced Wally and shook my finger. "Stay flat on the ground till we come back," I ordered.

This time, I thought his squeak sounded less sad.

———

When Marla and I returned to Rosinda with the branches and twigs, the witch chose a new spot to break the spell. "We're doing everything different just in case the hat doesn't like repeats," she explained.

After Rosinda lit the fire, she added six bottles of water and petals from a new red rose—from a different bush—to her pot and placed the filled pot on the flames. While the water boiled, I returned to the oak tree for Wally.

The giant rat was still lying motionlessly on the grass, just like I'd told him. "Good job," I said, patting his back. "We're just about ready."

Luckily it had started to drizzle, which reduced the number of people in the park. Otherwise, a girl accompanied by a seven-foot rat would have raised eyebrows. The light rain hadn't affected the fire because the water in the pot was bubbling.

"He's huge!" Rosinda exclaimed, eying the rat.

"And getting huger," I said. "Can you please break the spell now?"

Nodding, the witch placed the sorcerer's hat on her head and positioned herself next to Wally. "Oh, great and powerful magic hat," she chanted. "Please change Wally the rat to the real Wally Levitt, the twenty-year-old male person."

There was an immediate poof, followed by white smoke, and when the haze cleared, a stunned-looking Wally—the guy—stood next to the fire.

"You're back!" I hollered, rushing to him and throwing my arms around his shoulders.

Wally smiled and let me hug him.

"I'm so sorry," I continued. "But you're okay now, aren't you?"

"Squeak," Wally said, in his rat voice. "Squeak! Squeak! Squeak!"

"I give up!" I fell to the ground, shaking my head. "Why didn't the hat work?"

"Because magic is strong stuff," Rosinda said, throwing a bottle of water on the flames. "It doesn't always do exactly what you want." Taking off Aunt Jessie's hat, she pointed it at me. "That's why you shouldn't have messed with this."

"I know." I glanced at Wally, standing next to Marla, who was trying to comfort him. "What do we do now—build another fire?"

The witch shook her head. "Nah. That could make it worse. At least he's human."

"But he still sounds like a rat!" I shouted.

"What about speech therapy?" Marla suggested. "Couldn't that work?"

"Maybe," Rosinda said.

———

So that's what I did. After telling Wally's parents some unfortunate unknown experience had scared Wally so much that he could no longer talk, I found a good speech therapist—Dr. Marge Russoff—and paid for the sessions. (It was the least I could do.) Three months later, Wally started speaking again.

I know exactly when it happened because Dr. Russoff called me, confused by Wally's first words: "I hate Deb."

GEORGE'S MOTHER

George Demerest opened his front door Saturday morning and nearly fainted. "Mother?" he whispered.

"Oh, Georgie-Porgie," the woman squealed, throwing her arms around the much taller man. "I'm so glad to see you!"

Extricating himself from the woman's grasp, George took a step back. "You can't be here," he said. "You're dead. We buried you last month."

The woman smiled. "That was all nonsense—a terrible mix-up. As you can see, I'm perfectly fine."

George studied the woman who claimed to be his mother. She looked exactly like the late Sylvia Demerest. She had the same curly silvery hair, the same piercing gray eyes, the same wrinkled brow— even the same mole under her left eye. *But how could that be?*

"Can we go inside, Georgie?" the woman said. "Or are we going to stand out here all day?"

Opening the door behind him, George waved her forward. The woman stepped into the foyer, marched into the living room, and sat on the blue suede couch—smoothing the cushion the same way his mother always did.

George remained in front of the sofa, still examining the woman.

"Stop staring at me, Georgie. You're making me nervous."

"I'm making you nervous?" George shouted. "You're supposed to be dead! I saw your body inside the coffin!"

"A silly mistake."

"Mistake! You had a heart attack! You died! There was a big funeral—with all our relatives and your friends." George shook his head. "This can't be happening."

"Well, it is," the woman said. "I'm your mother, I'm alive, and I'm here."

"But how...? You've got to tell me how this happened. Dead people don't just walk out of their coffins and return to life."

The woman laughed. "I don't know what other dead people do," she said. "But that's exactly what I did."

For the first time, George looked at the clothes the woman was wearing and realized she was dressed in his mother's favorite outfit: the navy pantsuit he had buried her in.

———

The woman sat patiently, waiting for George to speak. "You said you stepped out of the coffin," he said. "When did this happen?"

"Just now—and I came right here." She chuckled. "I don't seem to have the keys to my apartment."

"You died. You don't have an apartment any more."

The woman sighed. "That's too bad. Then I'll have to live with you."

"I have to discuss that idea with Valerie first."

"Oh, her."

George winced. His mother had never approved of his wife. He sat quietly before speaking. "What was my father's name?" he finally asked.

"That's easy. George senior."

"What was his job?"

"He was a scientist at Blackstone Labs for thirty-five years."

Something harder..."What food do I hate the most?"

"Asparagus."

"Who was my first grade teacher?"

"Oh...I have to think about that one." The woman closed her eyes for a moment. "I remember now—Miss Barwin. She was short and chubby and laughed a lot."

George stared at the woman. "You seem to have all the answers," he said.

"That's because I'm your mother, Georgie."

"You can't be. It's not possible."

She shrugged and smiled. "Apparently it is possible because here I am."

———

George paced back and forth, wondering what to do. Glancing at his watch, he realized it was nearly eleven. Valerie would soon be home from the gym and he didn't want her to see the woman until he had a better grasp of who she was.

"Come on," he said, walking to the front door and holding it open.

"Where are we going, Georgie?"

"To the cemetery."

The woman frowned. "Why there?"

"I want to see your gravesite."

"There's nothing to see."

"Fine," George said. "Then I'll see nothing. Let's go."

Peacewood Cemetery was about a mile from George's house. The woman claimed to have walked the distance so George opted not to drive.

They walked in silence, the woman keeping up with George's brisk pace. "You walk very well for a person who just died of a heart attack," George finally said.

"But I didn't die."

"You deny having a heart attack?"

The woman shrugged. "Maybe I did; maybe I didn't. Whatever happened before doesn't matter since I feel perfectly fine now."

George didn't say anything else until they reached Peacewood Cemetery and continued to the spot where his mother had been buried, next to his father's headstone. Although the earth was fresh, it was neatly tamped down.

"It looks like nothing's been moved," George said.

"True," the woman agreed.

"But you told me you crawled out of the coffin."

"I did."

"Without upsetting the dirt?"

The woman laughed. "I fixed the grave, Georgie. I didn't want to leave it messy. Look at my shoes."

When George lowered his head, he saw the woman's shiny black pumps were heavily coated with soil.

———

They stood silently at the gravesite for several minutes, George unsure what to do next.

"Can we please leave?" the woman asked. "This place is creepy and like I told you, there's nothing to see."

"But there should be something—a sign that you crawled out of the coffin."

"I'm sorry, Georgie," the woman said, turning away. "I have no answers."

They walked back to George's house without exchanging another word. After he unlocked the door, the woman followed him inside, returning to the couch where she again smoothed the cushion.

"I don't know how to explain you to Valerie," he said, leaning against the wall.

The woman shrugged. "You won't have to explain anything. She'll recognize me and realize I'm your mother."

"You're not my mother!" George shouted. "My mother's dead! She died of a heart attack!"

The woman shook her head. "Then who am I?"

"An imposter."

"I must be a very good imposter, Georgie, because I look like your mother, act like your mother, and know things only your mother could know." She shrugged again. "But if you refuse to believe me, then we'll wait for your lovely wife."

———

George continued to lean against the wall until he heard a key turning the front-door lock.

"I'm home!" Valerie announced.

"Thank goodness," her husband said. "Please come in here."

"What's going...?" Valerie stopped talking and stared at the woman on the couch. "And who the hell are you?"

The older woman groaned. "You know very well who I am."

"No." The brunette in the red-striped jogging suit shook her sweaty head. "You're not her. Sylvia Demerest is dead and buried."

"Here we go again!"

Valerie looked at George. "This is some kind of scam," she said to him. "A horrible scam."

"I know," he agreed. "But she looks just like my mother and she answered questions about me that just my mother would know. She claims she stepped out of the grave and came here, but we went to the cemetery and it looks like nothing's been touched..."

"I told you I fixed the grave!" the woman shouted. "I really am Sylvia Demerest!"

"The hospital," Valerie said. "We'll take her to County Medical for an examination. They'll find out who she really is."

"I don't want to go to the hospital," the woman whined. "I'm not sick."

George moved next to her. "If you don't come with us, then you're leaving this house."

"You'd throw your mother out the door, Georgie?"

"You're not my mother!"

"All right," the woman said, standing. "Let's go to the hospital."

———

The bearded man behind the Admissions desk looked at George, Valerie, and the elderly woman and shook his head. "I don't understand why you're here," he said.

"I told you," George replied. "We need to have this woman tested."

The clerk pointed to the silver-haired woman. "She says she's your dead mother?" he asked.

"I *am* Sylvia Demerest," the woman insisted.

"No, you're not! My mother's dead!" George spoke so loudly that several people in the lobby turned and stared at him.

"You see what I mean?" George whispered to the Admissions clerk. "We need to find out who she really is."

"And how would we do that?"

"I don't know—a DNA test or something like that. Whatever you do to prove or disprove a person's identity. I've got some hairs from my mother's brush."

The man behind the desk stood and nodded. "Let me get someone who can help you."

———

The bearded clerk returned to the Admissions desk, accompanied by a stout African-American woman in a white lab coat, who extended her hand to George, Valerie, and the woman claiming to be George's mother. "I'm Doctor Templeton. Please come into my office so we can discuss your situation."

The trio followed the doctor into a small windowless cubicle. "Now tell me what this is about," Dr. Templeton said as she sat behind her desk.

George reviewed all that had happened since the woman appeared at his door.

After he finished, the doctor studied the older woman. "And you claim to be his mother, Sylvia Demerest?" she asked.

"That's who I am."

Turning to her computer screen, Dr. Templeton typed on the keyboard. "I've just confirmed that Sylvia Demerest died on April twenty-third of this year and was interred the following week, as Mr. Demerest said." She rested her elbows on the desk and cupped her chin. "So who are you?"

"Sylvia Demerest," the woman said. "Can't you do the tests like Georgie asked? That will prove who I am."

The doctor shook her head. "You can't be a dead woman."

"But I am."

Dr. Templeton looked at George. "I'd like to speak to her alone for a few minutes, so if you and your wife would please wait outside."

Valerie stood and George nodded. As they closed the door behind them, George looked at Dr. Templeton's nameplate. It read "Clinical Psychiatrist."

———

Dr. Templeton studied the older woman intently and she returned the psychiatrist's gaze. Finally, the doctor spoke. "Who are you really?" she asked. "You can tell me the truth."

The silver-haired woman chuckled. "I'm still Sylvia Demerest. My answer won't change."

"You really believe that?"

"It's the truth."

"You understand that Sylvia Demerest died several weeks ago and was buried in the ground?"

The woman shrugged. "I can't explain how I got here. I just know who I am."

Dr. Templeton shook her head. "I was hoping you would tell me what really happened."

"Georgie told you all that."

"I meant before you arrived at his door this morning."

"I don't know what happened before," the woman said. "I don't remember dying or being buried. I only know that I got out of the coffin and walked to Georgie's house."

The doctor stared at the woman again. "It's impossible to do that. People don't climb out of their graves."

"Maybe other people don't. But that's what I did."

Dr. Templeton rose and opened her office door. "Come back in," she told George and Valerie. "I didn't learn anything new so here's the plan. I'll do a cheek swab on our mystery lady for a DNA test and put a rush on it, but we still won't get the results for twenty-four hours. I'll be in touch when I have some answers."

———

"What are we going to do with her for a day?" Valerie whispered to George as they walked to the car, the older woman trailing behind them.

"I don't know."

"I'm hungry," the woman announced as she slid into the backseat. "I feel like I haven't eaten in days."

"About a month, actually," Valerie said.

"Where can we eat?" the older woman asked, ignoring Valerie's words. "How about that new Mexican restaurant?"

"Los Amigos?"

"Yes. Let's eat there."

George looked at Valerie, who shrugged. "Fine," he said. "We'll have lunch at Los Amigos."

———

In a cushioned restaurant booth, George and Valerie watched the woman opposite them devour her third cheese quesadilla. "You weren't kidding," George said. "You certainly were hungry."

The woman nodded as she continued to stuff food into her mouth.

"You got a free meal out of this charade," Valerie said, frowning.

The woman stopped eating and glared at George's wife. "I told you who I am," she whispered.

"Yes, you did. But it's not possible."

The older woman resumed eating while George and Valerie, who had finished their meals, continued to wait. Finally, the woman dabbed her mouth delicately with the cloth napkin and smiled at George. "I'm done. Are we going home now?"

Valerie turned to her husband, shaking her head ever so slightly.

The movement was enough for George to get the message. "You're staying at a hotel tonight," he said.

"Georgie?" the woman whined.

"I'm sorry, but until we know who you are, you can't stay with us," he explained.

Tears rolled down the silver-haired woman's cheeks. "You're my son, my only child, and you're sending me away." She pointed to her navy pantsuit. "I don't even have any other clothes—no comb, no toothpaste, no..."

"We'll buy the stuff you need," Valerie interrupted. "And you can cut the crying act because, no matter what you do, you're not sleeping in our house tonight."

———

George drove to the nearest mall and watched as the woman who claimed to be his mother chose several pairs of pants, tops, and underwear, plus the necessary toiletries. After Valerie added a black duffle bag, George paid for the items and they returned to the car.

"Drive to the Ramada," Valerie ordered as she removed the tags, folded the clothes, and placed the purchases inside the black bag.

"That's a motel, not a hotel," the woman in the back seat said. "I don't want to stay there."

"Where do you want to go?" George asked.

"If I have to spend the night in a strange place, can't it at least be a nice hotel?"

"Fine," Valerie said. She turned to her husband. "Drive to the Regency."

"That place costs a fortune," George whispered.

"It's just for tonight," Valerie said. "Tomorrow we'll get the DNA results."

———

"Today's been a nightmare," George said to Valerie as he drove home after checking the woman into the Regency and escorting her to a sixth-floor room with a spectacular lake view.

"As soon as we hear from the doctor, we'll be finished with her."

"I hope so. It's creepy because she looks and sounds so much like my mother."

Valerie shook her head. "Whoever planned this, did a thorough job. But you can't duplicate another person's DNA so all this work and plastic surgery was for nothing."

———

The Demarest's phone rang at eight o'clock the next morning. "When are you coming to get me?" the woman whined.

"We gave you enough money," George said, sitting up in bed. "Have breakfast in the hotel. It's Sunday and..."

"If you'd let me stay in your house, Georgie, then you wouldn't have needed to wake up early."

"All right. I'll be there as soon as I get dressed."

Valerie leaned on her pillow and frowned. "She's a lot like your mother, the way she bosses you around."

"What am I supposed to do?" George asked as he stepped into a pair of jeans.

"You could've let her stay at the hotel for another hour or so. She's not exactly suffering."

"I hope Dr. Templeton calls soon with those results."

"If we don't hear anything by three, I'm phoning her."

———

Dr. Templeton called at two-thirty. "You won't believe this," she began. "The woman's DNA matches the hairs you gave me — the ones you said belonged to Sylvia Demerest."

"That's impossible," George said. "My mother's dead. We saw her body, the casket, the burial..."

"I can't explain it, but bring her to the hospital tomorrow so we can do a thorough examination. If what you say is true, this woman is the medical story of the century."

"Story of the century," George repeated as he hung up the phone.

"I told you," the older woman said. She sat on the sofa, smoothing the cushion, nodding, and smiling. "But you wouldn't believe me."

"And I still don't believe you."

"Georgie, I am your mother. What else do I have to do?"

"I know," Valerie said. "We'll open the casket. Let's see what's in there."

The woman groaned. "You know what's in there—nothing, because I'm here."

"Then you won't mind us opening the casket," Valerie continued.

"Of course not. But it's just another a waste of time."

———

While Valerie gathered the necessary paperwork for exhuming Sylvia Demerest's body, George asked the woman claiming to be his mother more questions—"Who was my best friend in kindergarten? What's my favorite color? Who was my first date?"

The woman answered all his questions correctly and added details for each. "Paul Montague was your best friend, but you also liked Stevie Weinstein. Unfortunately, Stevie's mother wouldn't let him play with you or any of the kids because she was afraid Stevie would get sick. What a jerk she was."

At one point during the interrogation, George took Valerie aside. "How could anyone else know all this stuff about me?" he whispered. "I'm beginning to believe she really is my mother."

"It's impossible," Valerie said. "You know that."

"But the DNA..."

"It's some sort of trick, George—a really good one."

———

George and Valerie let the woman sleep in their house Sunday night. "It's too expensive to keep paying for a room at the Regency," George had argued.

"I don't trust her," Valerie had said.

"I don't trust her either, but we're taking her back to the hospital tomorrow morning anyway."

"Can we lock the guest room door?"

"No, but we can lock our door."

———

On Monday morning, instead of both going to work—George to Fine Foods, where he was an assistant manager and Valerie to Westhall Bank, where she was the mortgage officer—they drove their houseguest to County Medical.

After they identified themselves, two doctors immediately materialized—a short middle-aged Asian man and a ponytailed younger woman with glasses—and both enthusiastically shook the hand of the silver-haired woman.

"Where's Doctor Templeton?" George asked.

"The doctor had an emergency," the woman said, ushering their patient through the sliding-glass door.

"Can we come inside with her?" Valerie asked.

"We'd rather you stayed here," the male doctor replied, smiling. "It'll be more comfortable."

"The exam shouldn't take longer than an hour," his colleague added.

George and Valerie waited in the visitors' lounge. He spent the time skimming through various magazines while she fiddled with her phone. After forty-five minutes, George tossed a copy of *Men's Health* on the table and began pacing.

"Stop it," Valerie said. "You're making me nervous."

"They should be finished by now. It's nearly an hour."

The couple waited several more minutes. When nothing happened, George walked to the receptionist's desk. "What's the status of the examination, please? It's been more than an hour."

"Patient's name?" the auburn-haired woman asked.

"She says she's my mother, Sylvia Demerest, but that's not her real name."

"Then what's her real name?"

"That's what we're trying to find out."

"One minute please." The woman rose and continued to the next station, where a bald young man glanced at his computer screen. She said something to him, he pointed to the monitor and whispered to the older woman, who frowned and returned to her desk.

"What's wrong?" George asked.

"There's no patient listed with the name Sylvia Demerest."

"She's not really a patient. She's just here for a quick exam."

"Everyone seen by a doctor is entered into our system." The woman stared at George. "Are you sure a doctor took her inside?"

"Two doctors."

"What are their names?"

George shrugged. "I don't know. They didn't introduce themselves. One was an Asian man and the other was a woman with a ponytail and both were wearing white doctors' coats."

The clerk showed George photos of all the doctors on duty—and none matched the two people who had taken the woman who claimed to be Sylvia Demerest.

———

While George returned to the waiting room to explain the situation to Valerie, the clerk phoned Security. Several minutes later, a burly Hispanic man wearing a blue County Medical Center Security uniform approached the couple.

"You say two people impersonated doctors and took your mother?" the man asked.

"She's not my mother," George said, this time checking the man's nametag, which read Victor Robles. "My mother is dead so that woman is someone else."

Robles stared at George.

"All right," George said, sighing as he quickly filled the security guard in on what had happened and handed him a photo of his mother.

"Man, that's some weird shit."

"We know," Valerie agreed. "But what do we do now?"

"You two do nothing," Robles said, pointing to his chest. "Me and my staff, we'll check the hospital for those two and the older lady. I'll let you know what we find."

———

Robles returned to the waiting room an hour later. "Nothing, *nada*," he said, shaking his head.

"You couldn't find them?" Valerie asked, standing.

"Not a trace and nobody even remembered seeing any of them— the two in doctors' clothes or the old lady."

"So they just disappeared?" George said.

"I don't know what to tell you. The only video we have of them is when they took the woman from you. They must've left the hospital right away."

"And gone where?" George asked.

Robles shrugged. "Who knows?"

"What happens now?" Valerie asked.

"You can go to the police to report the old lady missing," Robles suggested.

"But we don't know who she really is," George pointed out.

"Since she's not your mother, you can forget about her," Robles said. "Just chalk it up as a bad dream." He held out his hand. "Sorry, I couldn't help and good luck."

As they watched the security guard leave, Valerie turned to her husband. "I think we should go ahead with our plans."

"Exhuming the body?"

Valerie nodded. "Let's make sure your mother's still buried in the casket."

———

George and Valerie didn't call the police and the woman claiming to be George's mother didn't contact them. However, on Wednesday afternoon they returned to the site of Sylvia Demerest's grave in Peacewood Cemetery where two men holding shovels stood next to an open hole.

George looked down and saw the top of his mother's casket. As he held Valerie's hand, one of the cemetery workers dropped into the hole and lifted the latch.

"What the hell?" the man shouted. "There ain't nothing in here!"

———

George and Valerie didn't talk during the short ride home.

"It's impossible," George said when they were inside their house. "This whole thing is impossible."

"I know," Valerie whispered. "But I've been thinking about something."

"What?"

"Your father...Wasn't he a research scientist?"

"Yes, but what does that have to do with all this?"

"Didn't he study cell regeneration?"

"You don't believe...?"

"George, I don't know what to believe. But what if your father discovered something at work and used it...?"

"My father died seven years ago," George interrupted, shaking his head. "Even if he knew something—which I'm sure he didn't—he couldn't have done anything now."

"But there's a woman with your mother's DNA who's alive and we just saw Sylvia Demerest's empty casket." Valerie looked at her husband. "What if those two people who took her were scientists from your father's company?"

"You think my mother was part of a medical experiment?"

"I don't know, but I think we should talk to the police."

———

"That's one hell of a story," Officer Powell said as he sat behind his desk facing George and Valerie. "Your dead mother came back to life and was abducted by two scientists?"

"I know it sounds crazy," George agreed. "But my mother's casket is empty and a woman who looks like my mother and has my mother's DNA disappeared from the hospital."

"But you didn't report that when it happened."

George sighed. "Because then we were sure she wasn't my mother."

"And now you're not so sure?" Officer Powell asked.

"Yes," George agreed.

The officer reached for a clipboard and pen. "Give me a description of the people who took her and we'll check them out along with that company your father worked for."

"Blackstone Labs."

———

"This whole experience is making me nervous," Valerie said as George drove home from the police station.

"You're nervous? It's my mother."

"We don't know that for sure."

"We don't know anything." He parked the car in the driveway and turned to his wife. "Val, what about Doctor Templeton? Isn't it strange that she never called to ask what happened?"

"I assumed the security guy told her."

"But what if he didn't? She was really interested in the matching DNA. Wouldn't she have followed up?" George reached for his phone and called the doctor's office. As he listened to the person on the other end, he nodded. "I see."

"What did they say?"

"Doctor Templeton's on vacation and won't be back for two

weeks."

———

George and Valerie, each holding a mug of coffee, sat at their kitchen table. "I'm getting a bad feeling," Valerie said.

"We should wait for Officer Powell's report."

"He won't find anything."

George frowned at his wife. "How can you be so sure?"

Valerie took a sip of coffee and then stood. "The people who planned this thing with your mother—they're getting rid of whoever's interfering with what they're doing."

"Like Doctor Templeton?"

Valerie nodded.

"But what about us? We're meddling too."

"Maybe they need us because of the connection to your mother."

———

When Officer Powell didn't call by Friday afternoon, George phoned the station.

"So?" Valerie asked when he got off the phone.

"Officer Powell wasn't in today and he was out yesterday too. He called in sick."

"I told you."

"A conspiracy?"

Valerie shrugged. "Something's going on—and the only clue we have is the Blackstone Labs connection."

"If the company's involved with the woman who says she's my mother, they won't let us in."

"Then we have to get in without their help."

George stared at his wife. "You want us to break into the lab?"

"What else can we do?"

"What if they catch us?"

Valerie smiled. "They won't. I have an idea."

———

Dressed in light blue uniforms with the name "Sanitary Cleaning Services," George and Valerie approached Blackstone Labs' reception desk.

"You're early," the young woman said, pointing to the clock on the wall. "It's not even five yet." She studied Valerie's face and then George's. "I don't remember seeing you guys before."

"We're new," Valerie explained. "That's why we're early—to get a head start and make sure we get everything cleaned."

"Okay, I guess," the girl said, studying her purple fingernails. "Go on in." She tapped a button, the buzzer sounded, and George and Valerie entered the inner confines of Blackstone Labs.

"Where do we go from here?" George whispered.

"We have to find the janitor's supply room," Valerie replied. "But it's okay to ask." She smiled at her husband. "Remember, we're new here."

———

Armed with a mop, sudsy bucket of water, and vacuum cleaner, George and Valerie inched along the tiled floors of Blackstone Labs. "Work slowly until the people leave," Valerie whispered.

George nodded.

At 5:30, when most of the employees had left, Valerie tapped George's shoulder and dragged the vacuum to a door marked "Restricted Area."

George turned the knob. "It's locked," he whispered.

Valerie took out the key ring she'd found in the janitorial closet. Her third attempt worked and the two of them guided the vacuum through the door.

"What are we looking for?" George asked.

"We'll know when we see it," Valerie replied.

With George pulling the vacuum canister, they walked past cubicles and lab tables, some with specimens and equipment, others housing cages with rats and mice. One skinny man in an oversized lab coat sat on a stool near a counter, writing in a notepad. He didn't acknowledge them.

George and Valerie continued to the back of the room, which contained an office. Valerie again took out the set of janitorial keys and tried each, but none unlocked the door.

Valerie motioned to the man still writing at the counter and headed to him. "Excuse me," she said. "We were told to clean the office in here, but our keys don't work."

Without looking up, the man reached into his lab coat pocket and produced a key. "Try this one," he said before resuming his writing.

Hurrying to the back, Valerie inserted the new key, which unlocked the door. Then she returned the key to the man, who nodded and continued to write.

———

George switched on the vacuum as he and Valerie entered the large office, which contained two massive desks, a file cabinet and bookshelf, in addition to an oval conference table with eight chairs.

"I don't see anything here that will help us find her," George shouted over the roar of the vacuum.

"We haven't even looked," Valerie said as she approached one of the desks. After starting the computer and discovering it required a password, she sifted through several folders and shook the pages of two books before turning to her husband.

"George!" she shouted. "Don't just stand there. Check the bookcase and see if anything seems wrong."

"What?"

"I don't know. Just look."

Valerie skimmed the contents of the file cabinet. Finding nothing unusual, she turned her attention to the second desk. Studying the jottings on a calendar blotter, she noticed a circled entry in the current week's "Monday" box.

"I think I found something!" she called.

When her husband reached the desk, Valerie pointed to the circle. "See?"

George nodded. The calendar entry contained the scribbled words "23 Pine Rd" followed by the initials "S.D."

———

According to the GPS, Pine Road was approximately five miles north. When they reached the location—a small house on a quiet suburban street—George turned off the lights and parked opposite.

"We can't just knock on the door," he said, "so what do you suggest we do?"

"Maybe go around to the back and see if there's an open door."

"Not likely."

"Do you want to call the police?" Valerie asked.

"I'm sure that won't work."

"Just sit here and wait?"

"At least for a while to see if anyone goes in or out."

"We should have brought a weapon."

"Valerie, that's nuts! We're not having a shootout here."

"I didn't mean a gun—but something to incapacitate them if they try to stop us from finding her."

"Like gas or a Taser?"

"Yes...Wait a minute. I may have something." Valerie opened her handbag and removed a small spray can.

"What's that?"

"Hairspray. It'll work if I zap them in the eyes."

———

George and Valerie sat in the car, watching and waiting. A half hour later, they heard voices and saw two men leave the cottage, lock the door, and drive away.

"Do you think there are more people inside?" George asked.

"Probably. But we should act now because we know for sure there're two less."

"And how do we get in?"

"Knock on the door and see what happens. If someone answers, act natural and if there's a problem, I'll spray them in the eyes."

George pounded on the front door while Valerie stayed hidden in the shadows. He heard footsteps and the door opened slightly.

"Yes?" a female voice asked.

"I'm looking for an elderly woman," George said. "I think she may be inside."

"No one else's here," the female voice said as she attempted to close the door.

Before she succeeded, George shoved the door open, knocking

the woman down. He and Valerie entered the house and looked at the person on the floor.

"It's her!" Valerie shouted, pointing her spray can towards the ponytailed woman with glasses. "You're the one who took her at the hospital!"

"Please let me explain," the woman said.

———

"This started many years ago," the woman began as she sat in the kitchen with George and Valerie hovering over her. "Your father and some other Blackstone Lab scientists had a theory about cell regeneration."

"My father?" George whispered.

The woman nodded. "It was a radical idea and they were never given permission to test it. In fact, they were ordered not to."

"But they experimented anyway," Valerie said.

"Yes, mostly with their own families. That way, the FDA wouldn't know. Whenever someone died, they would check if the person came back to life."

"You mean she really is my dead mother?" George gasped.

"Let me finish," the woman said. "Your father and the other early scientists were unsuccessful. None of their subjects' cells regenerated after death. However, the second wave of scientists including myself—I'm Eugenia Olsen—tweaked the formula, and your mother..." She shrugged. "Sylvia Demerest is our first success."

"But why her?" Valerie asked.

"Probably because she's been taking the pills for so many years."

"Did my mother know about this?"

Eugenia shook her head. "None of the subjects knew."

"She took this drug without knowing what it was?" George asked.

"The subjects were told they were getting special vitamins. They each took a daily pill."

"So you're saying that my mother got out of her grave and came to my door, just like she said."

"Yes, and we had no way of knowing until you brought her to

the hospital." She looked at George and sighed. "I'm sorry you had to be involved in all this, but we didn't think it would ever work and when it did, we had to test her."

"Couldn't you have explained this to us without kidnapping her?" Valerie asked.

Eugenia shook her head. "It wasn't my idea to do it this way."

"So where's my mother now? Can I see her?"

"In a minute, after I finish explaining."

_____

Eugenia stared at her hands without speaking.

"What is it?" George asked. "Is something wrong?"

The scientist nodded and raised her head. "She's failing and we don't know why."

"You mean my mother's dying again?" George grabbed Eugenia's arms. "Where is she?" he shouted. "I need to see her!"

"The bedroom on the right."

George ran through the hall and opened the door. A pale Sylvia Demerest, now wearing black pants and a gray sweater, lay on top of the bed, her eyes closed.

"Mother, I'm so sorry," George said, caressing the woman's cold hands. "I didn't believe it was you."

She opened her gray eyes and smiled. "Oh, Georgie-Porgie," she whispered. "I'm so glad you're here."

"How do you feel?"

"Tired...very tired."

"Mother, having you back is wonderful. Please don't leave me again."

"Georgie..."

He turned as Eugenia Olsen entered the room with Valerie. "Can't you do something?"

The scientist shook her head. "We haven't been able to locate the problem. Remember, your mother is our first successful revival."

"Georgie..." The voice was barely audible.

"Yes, Mother, I'm here." George grasped the woman's cold hand once more. "I'm so sorry..."

"Shh. I want to tell you how happy I was to be able to see you again. What a marvelous thing..." Her voice faded and then stopped.

Eugenia listened to the woman's chest and then turned to George. "Your mother is dead," she whispered.

——

George and Valerie buried Sylvia Demerest in the same casket in the same plot in Peacewood Cemetery, this time without any formal ceremony. The only mourners at the brief interment were Eugenia Olsen and several other Blackstone Labs scientists.

George and Valerie merely nodded to the scientists and afterwards the participants hurried back to their cars. As a result, none of them noticed the activity in Tranquility Lane, a nearby street in the cemetery. They didn't see Peter Saperstein quietly step out of his grave and walk towards the exit.

SKINNY ALEX

"I'm still too fat," Alex muttered as she examined herself in her bedroom's full-length mirror. Shaking her head, she turned and reached for the light switch.

"Wait!" a girl's voice called.

Alex stopped in mid-motion, her hand trembling. *Who's talking?* She was alone in the house.

"Don't be scared," the voice said. "Just look into the mirror again."

Slowly, Alex returned to the mirror and stared at her reflection. This time the image looked different. Yes, it was still her. But the girl in the mirror was thinner, the way she'd look if she lost about fifteen pounds.

"That's right," the soothing voice coming from the skinny girl in the mirror said. "I look terrific, much better than you."

Alex took a step back. This reflection couldn't be talking to her.

"It's not your imagination," Skinny Alex said. "I can talk to you — and even better, I can be you."

"Huh?" Alex stared at her thin self.

"It's easy," Skinny Alex continued. "All you have to do is put your hand into the mirror and pull me out. Do it and you'll look like this." She did a quick pirouette, showing off her svelte figure.

"But if you come out, what happens to me?" Alex asked.

"No problem. You'll stay inside the mirror."

"Then how will I know what's going on?"

Skinny Alex laughed. "I'm still you, silly, so you'll know everything I do—and you'll look great because you'll be thin. C'mon, let's trade places. You know you've always wanted to look like this—and now you can."

Tentatively, Alex touched the mirror and the glass rippled, creating a narrow opening. In an instant, her reflection grabbed Alex's hand and vaulted out of the mirror and into the bedroom.

"Thanks," Skinny Alex said, smiling as she picked up the backpack and turned off the light. "Time to go to school."

From inside the cold dark mirror, Alex watched her thin double leave and wondered what she had done.

———

"You look wonderful!" Alex's best friend, Lola, exclaimed as they stood side by side at their lockers, discarding coats and books. "What'd you do?"

"I found a new diet pill that takes off weight immediately," Skinny Alex lied.

"Really? And your parents let you do that?"

Skinny Alex shrugged. "I didn't tell them."

"Whoa!" Taking a step back, Lola stared at her friend. "That doesn't sound like you."

"I decided it's time for a change," Skinny Alex said.

Inside the mirror, Alex cringed and bit her nails.

———

As Skinny Alex took the history test, her perplexed double watched anxiously. *What's she doing?*

Alex's thin self spent more time looking across the classroom, trying to catch the attention of that cute guy, Seth, than answering questions about the Civil War.

When Mr. Broderick told the class to stop writing, Skinny Alex wasn't even holding her pen. She was still trying to flirt with Seth.

"Is everything all right, Alex?" Mr. Broderick asked when he picked up her paper and glanced at it.

"Everything is fine," Skinny Alex said, smiling.

"But you left most of the test paper blank."

"Sorry," Skinny Alex said.

She didn't look at all sorry, Alex realized. *What have I done?*

———

"You failed the test!" Alex yelled as soon as Skinny Alex approached the bedroom mirror.

"So what?"

"So I get 'A's in American History and I don't fail tests."

"You do now."

Alex leaned forward in the mirror, but couldn't push herself through. "I don't want to be in here anymore," she said. "Get back inside the mirror and let me out."

Skinny Alex shook her head. "No way. I'm having too much fun."

"Failing tests!"

"That's not important. Did you see how Seth, the guy you like, noticed me today?"

"Of course he noticed you! You flirted with him instead of taking the history test!"

"Yeah, and he flirted back. He even winked at me."

Alex pushed herself against the mirror. "Please let me out."

"Uh, uh."

"I'll tell Mom and Dad."

"Go ahead and try. No one else can see or hear you in there—just me."

Tears rolled down Alex's cheeks as Skinny Alex turned off the bedroom light.

———

The next day, Alex again could only helplessly observe the actions of her thin self. At lunchtime, she watched Lola approach her double in the school cafeteria.

"Hi, stranger," Lola said, sitting on the bench next to Skinny Alex. "I haven't seen you much this week."

"I've been busy."

"Really? Doing what?"

Skinny Alex shrugged. "Just making some new friends."

"Oh? Like who?"

"Saralynn and Marnie."

Lola stared at Skinny Alex. "Those girls? You never liked them before. All they do is run after boys and get into trouble. Marnie even failed English and Science last term."

"So what?" Skinny Alex said. "Getting all 'A's is boring and boys don't like smart girls. I want to have more fun."

"You think failing school is fun?"

"Maybe—especially if it gets Seth to like me...Oh, there he is." Skinny Alex jumped up and waved, pointing to the empty space on the other side of the bench.

Lola picked up her tray, shaking her head. "I thought you were my BFF," she said. "But you're acting so weird. Obviously you don't want to hang out with me."

Skinny Alex didn't answer Lola. "Seth!" she called instead. "There's plenty of room over here!"

———

"Now you're making my friends hate me!" Alex shouted as soon as Skinny Alex entered the bedroom.

"Lola? What's to like about her? She's such a wimp. Marnie's much more fun—and so is Saralynn."

"But I don't like those trampy girls!"

"Who cares who you like? They're my friends now and I like them a lot."

"Please..."

"You're a wimp too, always whining at me."

"I want to get out of the mirror. Let me out!"

Sklnny Alex shook her head. "Trading places was your decision. You wanted to be thin so you said I could be you."

"That was before you started ruining my life!"

"I'm not ruining anything. I'm making your life much better. Look at what's going on with me and Seth."

"You're chasing him."

"So what? He likes me."

"He just likes all the attention you're giving him."

Skinny Alex shrugged. "He never even looked at you and he ate lunch with me today."

"Because you practically dragged him to the table."

Skinny Alex walked to the door. "I don't have to listen to you."

"Please do your homework!" Alex called. But the only response she heard was a faint giggle.

———.

"Look what I have," Skinny Alex said as she entered the bedroom, waving a bunch of twenty-dollar bills.

"Where'd you get all that money?" Alex asked, knowing she wouldn't like the answer.

"From the kitchen drawer."

"That's Mom's secret stash. Did she say you could take it?"

"I didn't ask."

"Now you're stealing?"

Skinny Alex shrugged. "I wouldn't call it stealing. I prefer to think of it as borrowing."

"So you're planning to give the money back?"

"Maybe."

"What are you going to say when Mom asks you what happened to the money?"

"I'll say I don't know anything about it."

"You'll just lie?"

Skinny Alex waved her hands at the mirror. "You're such a boring goody-goody. Mom probably won't even notice the money's missing—and meanwhile I'll use it to have fun."

"What kind of fun?"

"You'll see."

———

A tattoo! Alex watched in horror from inside the mirror as her thin self—accompanied by her new slutty friends, Marnie and Saralynn—had a huge pink rose inked on her left shoulder.

I don't want a tattoo—and I hate pink! Alex fumed until she looked at the tattoo again. *Maybe...*

Then she watched the three girls walk to the multiplex and buy tickets for *Bloody Gore*, the new slasher movie her parents would never allow her to see. Skinny Alex used Mom's money to pay for everything, including large sodas and giant tubs of popcorn.

When the movie started, Alex turned away, unable to endure the continuous throat-slashings and body-choppings. But the screams from the axe-wielder's victims were so loud that she couldn't ignore the horrifying sounds.

Soon, she told herself as she huddled inside her dark enclosure. *This will be over soon.*

————

"Isn't it terrific?" Skinny Alex asked as she lowered her tee over her left shoulder to reveal the pink rose tattoo.

"It's horrible," Alex muttered.

"You don't like my tat? Too bad," Skinny Alex said giggling, "because there's nothing you can do about it."

"It's not just that I don't like the tattoo—and I don't—but it's not done right. The part of the flower you can't see, behind your shoulder, isn't filled in with pink. There's only an outline." Alex shook her head. "What a sloppy job."

Skinny Alex twisted her neck, trying to look at the hidden rose petal. "I don't believe you. Saralynn and Marnie were with me and if something was wrong, they would've told me."

Alex shrugged. "Maybe they just didn't care."

Skinny Alex placed her hand behind her back, attempting to push up her shoulder. "Damn it! I still can't see the part you're talking about." She inched closer to the mirror.

Extending her arm through the rippling glass, Alex grabbed the hand Skinny Alex held behind her back. Then, in one quick motion, Alex vaulted herself out of the mirror and onto the bedroom floor.

"You tricked me!" Skinny Alex shouted from within the mirror.

Alex stood, put her hands on her hips, and smiled. "So what are you going to do about it?"

"You can't leave me in here! I was having so much fun..."

"...ruining my life." Alex finished her angry reflection's sentence. "But here's the good news," she continued, walking to the door. "Now you'll have lots of time to enjoy your tattoo."

Before switching off the light, Alex turned to the mirror. "And by the way," she added, "the rose is perfect."

"507-9302"

Tina Scivoletti picked up the ringing house phone.

"507-9302," the male caller said, pronouncing each digit slowly in a robotic voice.

"Yes, that's my number. Who are you?"

There was a click as the man ended the call, leaving Tina with the annoying buzz of a dial tone. Frowning, she hung up the phone and pressed *69 to learn the mystery caller's identity. But the recorded message droned, "That number is private."

Puzzled by the episode, Tina leaned against her kitchen chair. It was eight-thirty on a Wednesday evening. *Who'd call me like that? Must've been a mistake.* Returning to the living room, she snuggled into the couch and resumed watching *Romancing the Stone.*

———

At work Thursday, Tina had no time to think about anything but her job. As a paralegal for Kramer & Westingham, a firm specializing in real estate law, her day was filled with researching land ownership disputes and drafting numerous documents. She loved the job and since her divorce three years earlier, was grateful for the frenetic pace.

Nevertheless, after thirteen years, the work was tiring and she was glad to go home afterwards to unwind and relax. Opening the front door of the small house Tina retained after her breakup with Ron, she collapsed into the kitchen chair and closed her eyes.

When the phone rang two minutes later, Tina automatically reached for the receiver. "Hello," she said.

"507-9302," the male voice droned, speaking with no inflection.

"Why are you calling me?" Tina asked.

"507-9302," the voice repeated.

She slammed the receiver into the cradle and ran from the kitchen.

When her house phone rang the following evening, Tina checked the Caller ID information before answering and wasn't surprised to see, "That number is private." But when she let the call go to voice mail, she was surprised that the man left a message: "507-9302," spoken in the same robotic voice. Nothing else.

———

"So every time he calls, all he says is your phone number?" Jill asked as she drizzled raspberry vinaigrette on her salad. Jill was Tina's best friend and also her Saturday night dinner date.

Tina nodded.

"And it's been happening every day?"

"Yeah, since Wednesday, and it's creeping me out."

Jill shook her head, cascades of long blonde curls swinging back and forth. "If it doesn't stop, maybe you should go to the police and have them check the number. It could be a crime, like harassment."

"You think?"

"I don't know, but it's worth finding out." She took a bite of lettuce and pointed to Tina with her fork. "This is supposed to be a fun girls night out, so enough of the phone stuff. Let's talk about something else...Did you find anyone on that new dating site?"

———

The man phoned again Sunday, Monday, and Tuesday nights, each time only reciting Tina's number. On Tuesday, she recorded the man's call on her cellphone and the next day after work, drove to the police station.

"...and that's it," she concluded, playing the message for Officer Mason, a sympathetic African-American man in his fifties. "He calls me every night like this and it's very disturbing."

"Okay," the policeman said, looking up from the form he had been filling out. "I'll check last week's calls to your number, monitor incoming calls, and let you know what I find."

"When will I hear from you?"

Officer Mason smiled at her. "I'll get back to you as soon as I have a chance to review the records, probably sometime tonight."

———

True to his word, Officer Mason phoned Tina Wednesday evening. "We didn't find any calls made to your house from a private number," he said.

"That's impossible."

"Ma'am, I checked the records myself—every call you received since last Wednesday. The phone company supplied the log and if you don't believe me, I'll be glad to email it to you."

Tina sighed. "I'm sorry. I believe you, but I don't understand why those creepy calls aren't showing up. How can someone do that?"

"Maybe he's connecting to your phone and tapping the wire. But he's not threatening you in any way, is he?"

"No, but it's still very upsetting, so can you check the connection?"

The officer paused before responding. "Give me your address again and I'll be there tomorrow morning."

———

"He called me last night," Tina told Officer Mason when he arrived at her house at eight-thirty. "Maybe it has something to do with this old phone." As she touched the coiled cord of the black wall-mounted phone, Tina remembered Ron talking about replacing it with a modern cordless model. But he had never gotten around to doing that—along with many other things.

"The age of your phone doesn't matter, just the wiring," the officer said. "Now let's see if we can find out how he's calling you." After carefully examining the phone, he followed the wire along the wall to the outside connection and checked the hookup to the telephone pole.

When he returned several minutes later, Officer Mason shook his head. "There's nothing wrong with your phone or your phone line and he hasn't tapped it."

"Then how is he calling me?"

"Damned if I know," the policeman said. "Whatever's going on here is strange, I agree, but it's not criminal since all he's doing is repeating your phone number, not making any threats. Either bear with it or try taking the phone off the hook for a while and see if that stops the calls."

———

When she returned home from work, Tina did what Officer Mason suggested, resting her phone receiver and the attached cord on the kitchen chair. Although the buzzing noise was annoying, Tina found it preferable to the caller's creepy voice.

After dinner, she settled into the couch to watch a rom/com—*Pretty Woman*. Just before nine o'clock, near the movie's fairy-tale ending, her cellphone rang. She picked it up from the glass cocktail table and without checking the number, took the call.

"507-9302," the robotic male voice said.

"Who are you and what do you want?" Tina shouted.

She heard a click as the man ended the call.

Tina marched into the kitchen and slammed the house phone's receiver back in its holder. When the dial tone returned, she called the police and left a message for Officer Mason.

———

Tina was surrounded by legal documents at work late Friday morning when her iPhone rang. "I'm sorry that guy got your cell number too," Officer Mason said after she recounted the previous night's incident. "But he's still not doing anything criminal."

"Calling me every day—now on my cellphone too—that's not against the law?"

"He didn't threaten you, did he?"

"No."

"Then what he's doing isn't a crime in this state." The officer hesitated. "I didn't find any suspicious calls in the phone log. Are you sure...?"

"I played you the recording!" Tina shouted. "I'm not imagining all this!"

"Calm down," Officer Mason said.

"I need these calls to stop. What can I do?"

There was a pause again at the other end. "I don't have a solution, just a suggestion. Let the phone ring each time until it goes to voice mail and then, if the guy leaves a message, erase it. He may get tired of this game if you stop picking up the phone."

"Thank you," Tina said. "I'll try it."

———

When her house phone rang shortly after eight o'clock Friday night, Tina ignored the call. But this time the answering machine didn't pick up after the fifth ring and the telephone continued to ring and ring and ring. When she could no longer stand the noise, Tina lifted the receiver.

"507-9302," the robotic voice droned, followed by silence.

Instead of screaming at the phone, Tina held the receiver next to her ear and said nothing.

The silence at the other end of the line continued.

Tina held the phone to her ear for several minutes, but the caller didn't speak. "What do you want?" she finally whispered.

She heard a click, followed by the dial tone.

Tina grabbed her iPhone and punched in the 507-9302 house number. After the fifth ring, the answering machine picked up the call.

———

"I can't explain what happened," Officer Mason said when Tina reached him the next morning. "Maybe call your phone company and find out if there's a technical problem."

"Do you think that's what's going on here?"

"No."

Tina paused. "You think I'm making all this up, don't you?"

"I didn't say that..."

"Fine. I'll try the phone company." After ending the call, Tina punched in Verizon's number.

Adrienne, the customer service rep, listened without interrupting. "Wow!" she said when Tina finished. "That's some story. But while you were talking, I looked over your records and didn't find any unusual activity within the last month."

"Could a technician check my phone line, just to make sure it's okay?"

"Didn't you say you also got a call from this guy on your cell?"

"Yes."

"Then it can't be a problem with your landline connection, right?"

Tina sighed. "I guess not."

"Sorry, hon," Adrienne said. "I don't know what's wrong, but according to what I'm seeing, everything's working okay on our end. Good luck getting rid of your mystery caller."

———

Since it was Saturday, Tina did her grocery shopping and two loads of laundry. She had another girl-date with Jill scheduled for the evening—dinner and a movie—but didn't feel up to it.

"What's wrong?" Jill asked when Tina called to cancel.

"That creepy guy on the phone is really getting to me."

"He's still calling you?"

"Yes."

"Even more reason to get out of the house tonight."

"Okay, but just for dinner. I haven't been sleeping well so let's forget the movie."

"How about I come back to your house after we eat? Then, if the guy calls, I'll be there."

"Thanks, Jill. I can use the support."

———

"So when does the creep usually call?" Jill asked when they arrived at Tina's home.

"Mostly between eight and nine."

"And he just says your phone number?"

Tina nodded.

Jill leaned back against the fluffy couch cushions. "That doesn't sound so bad as long as he doesn't talk dirty or curse you out."

"It's still bad. Don't forget, he called my cell once and another time the phone wouldn't stop ringing." Tina shook her head. "It's messing with my mind. I'm having trouble concentrating at work too."

Jill picked up the remote and turned on the television. "We're not talking about that guy any more. We didn't go to the movies, but we're going to see one now."

They watched *When Harry Met Sally* without interruption. At ten-thirty, Jill grabbed her coat and pocketbook and kissed Tina goodbye. "See?" she said. "I'm good luck for you. The creep didn't call."

"The night's not over yet."

"Forget about him and go to sleep," Jill said as she walked out the door.

Five minutes later, the phone rang.

Tina didn't answer, but the machine didn't pick up the call and the ringing continued. When she could no longer stand the noise, Tina lifted the receiver.

"507-9302," the man said.

———

When Tina woke up late the next morning—a lazy Sunday with nothing planned—she disconnected the house phone and turned off her cell.

For nearly an hour, she read a mystery novel. But her mind kept returning to the creepy phone caller. *Did I get rid of him?* It wasn't even afternoon and the man didn't call until nighttime so it was too soon for self-congratulations.

She decided to drive to the mall—buy a shirt, maybe a pair of sneakers. Out of habit, she tossed the iPhone in her shoulder bag, but didn't turn it on.

As Tina wandered in and out of various stores—purchasing two tops, a purse, and a pair of dressy jeans—the only phones that rang were other people's cells. After buying a copy of *Entertainment Weekly*, she ate a late lunch in the food court, reading the magazine in the midst of noisy conversations and shrieks of young children.

After lunch, Tina bought a ticket to *Uncovered Leaks*, the spy thriller she was supposed to have seen with Jill. The movie was okay—not great—and her mind occasionally drifted back to the disturbing phone calls.

When the film ended, Tina returned to the food court for a cup of coffee and sat, again reading *Entertainment Weekly*.

"The mall will be closing in ten minutes."

Tina heard the announcement and checked her watch, realizing it was nearly six o'clock, Sunday closing time. After tossing her cup into the wastebasket, she carried her packages to the car and drove home.

———

That night, Tina left her house phone disconnected and her cellphone off. Switching on the TV, she watched a reality show rerun—teens climbing a steep mountain in some faraway country—fighting with each other and endangering themselves in the process.

One girl had fallen by the edge and was hysterically calling for help when Tina's iPhone rang. She looked inside her handbag and saw the "private number" message flashing. Without answering, she tried to again turn off the phone, but the ringing didn't stop. Even when she reset the phone to vibrate, the ringing continued. Finally, she answered the call.

"507-9302," the monotone male voice said.

"Leave me alone," Tina whispered.

The phone went dark, appearing to be off.

Tina huddled in the couch, her arms wrapped around her legs. She was in the same fetal position ten minutes later when the house phone rang.

Slowly, she got up and entered the kitchen. The receiver still lay on the chair in its cradle, disconnected from the phone wire. Nevertheless, the telephone continued to ring and the answering machine didn't pick up the call.

"No!" Tina screamed, hurling the receiver against the wall.

The impact made a small circular dent, but had no effect on the phone, which kept ringing. Tina lifted the receiver with its dangling cord, and held it against her ear.

"507-9302," the voice droned.

Tina reattached the phone and cradle to the wire in the wall. The phone immediately rang again and she picked it up after the first ring. "Stop it!" she screamed.

"Goodbye," the man's voice said.

Puzzled by the caller's new message, Tina frowned as she attempted to hang up the receiver. But the cord began to move, swaying independently under her arm. Then, slithering like a live snake, the looping coils wrapped themselves around her neck.

"No!" Tina gasped, trying to pull off the cord. But the coils tightened until Tina went limp, slumping to the floor.

———

"683-7144."

Mark Gershon didn't recognize the voice of the male caller. "That's the number here," he said. "Who are you?"

He heard a click followed by the dial tone.

Must've been a wrong number. Shaking his head, he hung up the bedroom phone.

WRONG ROAD

Did I remember to defrost the chicken?

The question popped into Wendy Jaraslaw's head as she drove to work, taking her concentration away from Route 35 for just a moment. But when her attention returned to the road, she was perplexed by what she saw.

The highway looked different. Wendy had driven this route for seven years—a 30-minute commute to her job as office manager for a construction firm—and she was so familiar with the trip that she'd joked to friends she could drive it with her eyes closed.

Although her eyes hadn't been closed, her mind had drifted and now Wendy was confused. *Where's the sign for the Cedarville exit?*

And the scenery was wrong. This was a suburban stretch so houses and shopping complexes should have lined the road. But they didn't. This road was flanked by trees and open meadows with several cows.

And the traffic. There wasn't any. According to the clock, it was 8:11—rush hour—yet hers was the only car. She looked for a sign identifying the road, but saw none.

Another highway? Wendy didn't understand how she could have tuned out enough to make such a major mistake. But that's what must have happened she decided as she watched for the next exit.

———

Wendy drove for what seemed like an unusually long stretch without an exit for a suburban highway. Although she passed a few scattered houses, most of the landscape remained undeveloped with no stores or commercial complexes. When a red exit sign finally appeared, she didn't recognize the name: Holmesboro.

Wendy exited the highway and then entered the same road in the opposite direction, figuring it would take fifteen minutes to get back to Route 35. *I can still be on time...*

The road was empty in this direction too, which made no sense. But Wendy ignored the weirdness as she drove quickly—well above the speed limit—something she never did. Again she passed green meadows with cows, clumps of trees, a few brightly colored homes, and not much else. She saw one exit and then another, but none looked familiar or connected to her highway.

When she looked at the clock again, the time still read 8:11. Frowning, she slowed the car and pulled off the road.

———

Wendy punched in her company's phone number and waited for someone to pick up. Sid would be in by now, Kelvin too. But the phone rang and rang without going to voice mail.

Closing the phone, Wendy plugged in her GPS. "How can I be lost?" she muttered as she entered the address of S & L Construction and waited for the woman's voice to guide her back to the correct road. But the machine went dark and when she tried to restart it, the power remained off.

She tried her phone's GPS, which she didn't like as much, but couldn't get a signal. Shaking her head, Wendy reentered the empty road and continued driving.

———

The next exit sign was for Bench Corners, a name she'd never heard before. Nevertheless, Wendy drove off the highway in search of a gas station, convenience store—some place with a person who could give her directions.

Again the area was sparsely populated and she saw no businesses, just a sprinkling of brightly colored homes. Pulling into the driveway of a small orange clapboard house, Wendy rapped lightly on the front door. When no one answered, she banged heavily, but got no response. After giving the door a final punch, she returned to the car and drove in the opposite direction.

She still didn't see another auto and the unnatural quiet made her jittery. At the next house—an emerald green ranch—Wendy parked and slammed the car door, mostly to hear the noise. Then she rushed to the entrance and rang the bell over and over. But the results were the same.

Returning to the car, Wendy sat quietly, tears trickling down her cheeks.

———

"What's the matter, lady?"

When Wendy looked up, she saw an elderly man with a heavily lined face staring at her. Opening the window, she asked, "Where am I?"

"Bench Corners."

"But I've lived here all my life and never heard of Bench Corners."

The man chuckled. "It's kind of a small place."

"Somehow I got off Route Thirty-Five," Wendy continued, stepping out of the car. "I'm late for work and need to find my way back. Can you please tell me how?"

The old man rubbed his chin before speaking. "Don't know if I can, Miss."

"If you don't know the way to the highway, maybe someone else can help me."

"I'm afraid that's not the problem," he said.

Wendy stared at the man, dumbfounded. "Then what is the problem?" she asked.

"The road you mentioned being on before," he said, shaking his head. "There's no Route Thirty-Five."

"What do you mean?"

"Your highway doesn't exist here."

"That's impossible. I just drove from Thirty-Five onto this road, whatever it's called. I didn't see a sign with its name or number."

"That's because it's the only big road so we call it 'The Road.' Not too clever, huh?" He chuckled.

Wendy didn't laugh. "Where am I really?" she whispered.

"I told you, Bench Corners."

"But it's not near any places I know...Am I dreaming?"

The man's expression became serious again. "No," he said. "Let's find a place to sit and I'll try to explain."

———

Wendy and the old man walked to an orange bench along the road and sat.

"It's happened before," the man began. "People like you getting off a road and ending up in The Land."

"But you said this isn't a dream and there's no Route Thirty-Five—so where am I?"

"I'm not sure what you'd call The Land—maybe another universe, another dimension—another place altogether."

"You're not part of the real world?"

"Oh, we're part of a real world—just not your world."

Wendy sat quietly. "Then how do I get back?" she whispered.

The man shook his head and spoke just as softly. "Now that's the problem." Then he smiled at Wendy. "The Land isn't a bad place to be in. You might like it here."

"I'm sure this is a wonderful place," Wendy agreed. "But I've got a family—a husband and two children who need me—so I have to go home. There must be a way."

"Well..." The man rubbed his wrinkled forehead.

Wendy forced herself to be patient as she waited for him to speak.

"There was one fellow who was able to go back," he said.

"So it can be done."

"But that fellow was lucky to find it."

"What...what did he find?" Wendy gripped the seat tightly.

"An opening—the way you got into The Land. If you find an opening, then you can get back."

"But I don't know where I got off my highway and onto yours," Wendy said, relaxing her fingers. "It just happened."

The man nodded. "That's why it's so hard to return to your world. The openings—they're very small and shift around."

Wendy thought for a moment. "You mentioned other people from my world getting stuck here. Can I talk to them? Maybe they know something that'll help me."

"You can try," the man said. "But remember, those are the folks that haven't been able to get back."

———

The man gave Wendy directions to a place where she'd find others who had become trapped in The Land.

"A hotel?" she asked.

"I don't know that word," he said. "This is just a house where folks get together."

"Like a meeting hall?"

"Maybe—but a small one," he said, smiling. "Everything here is small compared to where you're from. I'll let them know you're coming."

Following the man's directions, Wendy drove a short distance to another unnamed street, which she took for about a mile until she reached a gold house with a large "WELCOME" sign taped on the door.

After she knocked and no one answered, Wendy twisted the knob and stepped inside.

———

"Is anyone here?" Wendy called from the hallway.

"Be right down!" a woman's voice shouted.

Wendy entered a large room with two green sofas and several orange chairs positioned around an octagonal wooden table with yellow napkins and matching spork plastic utensils—spoons on one end and forks on the other. Wendy sat on one of the couches, picked up a spoon-fork, and twirled it in her fingers.

"Odd, isn't it?" the woman entering the room asked.

Looking up, Wendy met the eyes of a smiling brunette in her fifties, wiping her hands with a pink towel.

"That's the preferred silverware—or I should say plasticware because I haven't seen any metal cutlery. And they like bright colors." She dangled the towel in one hand and pointed to the neon green sofa with her other.

"You're from the U.S.?"

The woman nodded. "I'm Selena McDermitt from Los Angeles."

"Wendy Jaraslaw from Jamestown, Ohio—near Dayton...How did you get here, Selena?"

"Like you, I slipped through an opening, hole, rift, tear, seam— whatever you want to call it—and ended up in The Land."

"When did it happen?"

"About two years ago."

Wendy leaned against the back of the couch and sighed. "Were you driving?" she asked.

Selena shook her head. "I was walking my dog in the park and Scruffy broke loose so I chased him, following his barks. When I heard him right next to me, but didn't see him, I reached out and..." She spread out her hands and shrugged. "Here I am."

"You couldn't get back?"

Selena sat in the orange chair opposite Wendy and shook her head again. "The problem is that I thought I was still in the park. The scenery looked the same—more trees, trails, and lawns. And Scruffy was with me so we continued our walk. By the time I realized I was somewhere completely different and tried to retrace my steps, the opening was gone."

Wendy covered her eyes with her hands. "I need to go home," she whispered.

———

Selena was quiet for a moment. "I don't know if you can," she finally said.

"But the man I met told me someone went back."

"Yes, that's true." Selena nodded. "But Charles was extraordinarily lucky. The rest of us are living here and it's a good place."

Wendy stared at Selena. "You're not trying to go back to L.A.?" she asked.

Selena rose, walked to Wendy, and sat next to her. "Let me explain," she said. "My life in California wasn't great. I'd just divorced my cheating husband, was working as a waitress in a diner, and living in a dump. No kids, no close family, just a few friends and Scruffy—and Scruffy's with me."

"What do you do here?"

"This house with the 'Welcome' sign? It's my home and I'm the welcoming committee for people like you who fall through the opening."

"Are there many of us?"

"Thankfully, no. You're the fifth person since I came."

"Don't any of them want to leave?"

"Most do," Selena said. "In fact, one man—Bill Weston—should be here soon."

———

Selena's words were followed by a knock on the door. "Come in!" she called and a tall African-American man with a trim beard and mustache entered the room. "I was just talking about you, Bill," Selena said.

"Saying only good things, I hope," he said, smiling at Wendy. "I assume you're the latest visitor to this strange little world...Welcome."

"Thank you. I'm Wendy Jaraslaw. Selena said you want to get back home. Do you have a way? I really need to leave."

Bill sat on the couch opposite the two women and cupped his hands. "If I'd perfected a method, I wouldn't still be here," he said. "But I'm trying."

"Maybe I can help you," Wendy suggested. "If we work together..."

"Perhaps," Bill said. "But I've been working with Greta and Pablo and we haven't succeeded."

"How long have you been trying to get back?"

"Since the minute I arrived in The Land—and that's nearly seven months ago."

Wendy felt her eyes tearing. *Amber...Sean...Tommy.* "My family..." she mumbled.

"I know," Bill said. "I've got a wife and daughter in Michigan who have no idea where I went." He bit his lip. "They probably think I left them on purpose."

"So there's no way to communicate?" Wendy asked although she already knew the answer.

Selena shook her head.

"It's not so bad here," Bill said. "A little wacky, but peaceful—just kind of boring."

Wendy stood and faced Bill. "I really need to get back soon—not in months or years—so please show me what you're working on."

———

Bill's car was royal blue and tiny—just a two-seater—a model Wendy had never seen. "What a strange car," she said, opening the door.

Bill nodded. "After I walked through an opening into this world—the people here gave me the car."

"That was nice of them."

"Most of the natives don't drive," he said, shrugging. "They walk or ride bikes. It's not a big place."

"How big is it?"

"I'd guess it's the size of one of our smallest states—like Delaware."

"Are there oceans?"

"No, just lakes and rivers."

"Does this world have a name other than The Land?"

Bill chuckled. "That's what everyone calls it."

Wendy looked out the window as Bill drove on what the old man called The Road. There still wasn't much to see other than several colorful houses and acres of undeveloped land. Traffic was practically nonexistent. They passed a few cars and five or six bicycles until Bill exited at Moreway Station and turned right onto a smaller street.

"Where are we going?" Wendy asked.

"To our place. It's got a little laboratory. That's where we're experimenting, trying to find a way home."

―――

Bill parked the small blue car in front of a lemon yellow house and Wendy followed him inside. "I'm back with the new arrival!" Bill called.

A moment later, a smiling young woman with a blonde ponytail and dirty apron stepped into the orange hallway. "Hello," she said in lightly accented English. "I'm Greta Eriksson from Sweden. Sorry, I am not so clean." She lifted two smudged hands.

"Greta and I are looking for a chemical solution," Bill explained.

"I'm Wendy Jaraslaw from Ohio and I didn't know people got here from other parts of the world."

"Oh, yes." Greta nodded her head up and down. "The hole moves or maybe there are more openings." She shrugged. "We do not know how it happens."

"How long have you been here?" Wendy asked.

"Nearly one year."

Wendy felt her eyes start to water again. "Are you close to finding a way to get back?" she asked.

Greta shook her head. "Nothing I do is good."

―――

Wendy followed Bill and Greta to the living room lab. An assortment of sealed jars, bottles, and tubes filled a table and a crude hand-drawn map, divided into numbered sections—some of them marked with checks—covered the rear wall.

"This is it?" Wendy asked, unable to hide her disappointment.

"I know it doesn't look like much," Bill said. "But this world isn't big on science..."

"...or education," Greta added. "They learn only how to read and write and count."

"The map?" Wendy pointed to the back wall.

"Pablo made that himself," Bill said. "They don't care about geography either."

"What do they care about?" Wendy asked.

"Their families, their homes, happiness—things like that," Bill said.

"Very nice people in The Land," Greta added. "So kind."

"I guess that's why Selena wants to stay," Wendy said. "But I don't care how nice everyone is here. I have to get back."

Greta nodded. "I want to go home too. I try, but..." She spread out her arms.

"We will succeed," Bill said, striking the table with his hand.

————

After Bill drove Wendy to Bench Corners to retrieve her car, she watched Greta and Bill work in the lab. But her science knowledge was minimal so she wasn't able to help.

Lunch was cheese sandwiches on a tasty bread she'd never eaten before. "A rye-blend," Bill explained.

Following lunch, Wendy opted to go for a drive. "Anything I should know?" she asked Bill when she told him her plans.

"Not really," he said, chuckling. "You'll just see more of the same. But stay on The Road because it's easy to get lost, although the natives know where our house is so they'll be happy to guide you back."

*Boring...*The word kept popping into Wendy's head as she drove along The Road, joined only by a few cars and bikes. As Bill said, the scenery looked the same everywhere: colorful houses, a smattering of shops—a "Store Center" according to the sign—and lots of open space.

————

At twilight, a stocky man with glasses, holding a shoebox-sized metal machine, entered the lab house.

"Pablo, meet Wendy from Ohio," Bill said. "She just got here."

"Welcome and sorry," Pablo said, his words tinged with a Spanish accent.

Wendy pointed to the gray device. "What is that?" she asked.

"It checks the air," Pablo explained. "If something is different, the machine will beep."

"You mean if you find an opening—the way back to our world?"

"Yes."

"Can I help?" Wendy asked.

"Only if I make another air tester."

"Can you make me one, please?" Wendy asked, her voice cracking.

"It is tiring work," Pablo said. "I walk all day."

"I can walk too. I need to go home."

Pablo nodded. "We all need to go home. I will make a machine for you tonight."

———

After joining Bill and Greta for a macaroni and cheese dinner—cheese, not meat, being the preferred food—Wendy assisted Pablo, handing him the necessary tools as he constructed a second air-testing machine.

"I am so glad you will check the air with me," he said. "You are the first."

"Really?" Wendy said. "I'm surprised no one else wanted to do it."

"You must be outside all the time, walking. The others do not believe so much in this," Pablo said, shrugging.

"Selena said I'm the fifth person she's seen come here from our world and I've met three. Who's the other one?"

"A child," Pablo said. "Maria is nine years of age so she is living with a family."

"Is Maria happy here?"

Pablo shrugged again. "Who can be sure? I hope she is happy. She smiles when I see her."

Wendy thought of her own children¬—Amber was eight, nearly the age of the little girl trapped here, and Sean was just eleven. "Will the machine be ready for tomorrow?" she asked.

"Yes," Pablo said as he screwed two pieces together. "I will work until it is done."

———

After a restless night, the result of sharing a bed with Greta, Wendy ate breakfast with the others. "When can we get started?" she asked Pablo as she gobbled a buttered slice of the blended rye.

"Very soon," he replied. "I will finish my coffee and then we can leave."

Wendy had taken a sip of the coffee with her spork and disliked the bitter aftertaste. "I'll wait for you," she said, excusing herself.

Ten minutes later, she and Pablo left the house, each equipped with a whistle and an air-testing machine. But only Pablo carried a pager. He hadn't had enough time to assemble one for her. "I will make you a pager tonight," he had promised.

"Where are we going?" Wendy asked over the hum of the devices.

"I finished Section Twelve yesterday so we will start in Thirteen."

"How far until we get there?"

"A little more than one mile," Pablo said. "But the weather is good for walking."

Wendy, who hadn't thought about the temperature, realized it was comfortably mild, about seventy degrees and sunny. Glancing at the sky, she noticed that this world's sun, although bright yellow, wasn't totally round. It was slightly oval.

"You do this every day?" Wendy asked as they walked.

"Yes, since I made the machine, because I want to go home and I think this is the best way."

"How long have you been here?"

"It is five months now, much too long."

"Where do you live?"

"I am from Mexico, but I have lived in Yuma, Arizona for fifteen years."

"You have a family?"

Pablo nodded. "A wife and two boys. They are twelve and seven."

"I've got a husband and two kids nearly the same ages," Wendy said as they reached the testing area. "Tell me what to do so we can return to our families."

"You walk to the left and I will go to the right," Pablo said. "Listen to the machine. If something is different, the machine will beep."

"What happens if I hear a beep?"

"You blow the whistle and I call the others." Pablo indicated the pager on his belt.

"And everyone comes running?"

Pablo nodded.

"Will it work?" Wendy asked. "Will the opening stay there long enough for all of us to go through?"

"I do not know," Pablo said. "I have not found an opening yet."

"Do we wait for everyone?"

"No," Pablo said. "I call—and then we go through."

Wendy noticed a group of trees to her left. "Do I go into the woods?" she asked.

Pablo shook his head. "I am sure the hole is not there," he said. "Where were you when you came through?"

"Driving my car."

"I was walking behind my home," Pablo said. "Everyone came here from open land outside—no woods."

"How do I know when I'm finished?" Wendy asked. She wished they could use a time signal, but their watches didn't work here. Hers still read 8:11.

"Look for the big stick I put in the ground. That is the end of Section Thirteen. You will see a pink house. Go there and ask the kind people to drive you to the strangers' house." Pedro smiled. "You will be very tired."

———

It was boring work, just walking and listening to the steady droning of the machine and seeing nothing but grassland or an occasional tree. Wendy's legs became weary as she continued moving left, hearing nothing but the hum. Not even a bird interrupted the noise.

After stopping for a quick lunch—a cheese sandwich she had prepared at breakfast— Wendy again walked to the left with the air-tester in front of her, accompanied by the soft humming noise. With nothing interesting to look at, she thought about her family—Tommy and the kids—and what they would be doing in the early afternoon. Sean and Amber would be in school and Tommy would be...

The machine's hum changed to a steady stream of beeps. Wendy stopped daydreaming, placed the device on the grass and without moving her feet, waved her arms in all directions, searching for an opening like the one she'd fallen through.

"Pablo!" she called and then blew her whistle as loud and hard as she could, hoping he was close enough to hear her signal.

The machine still beeped steadily, but Wendy didn't feel anything different so, very slowly, she took a step forward and extended her left arm again. This time, part of the arm along with her hand disappeared.

Wendy blew her whistle once more. "Pablo, I found it!" she yelled. "Come here now!"

But there was no answer.

The beeps changed, becoming softer and less frequent. When Wendy looked at her outstretched arm, she saw more of it than before. "Pablo, I can't wait!" she yelled. "The hole's closing!" While she continued to blow the whistle, Wendy forced the rest of her body through the narrow opening.

She still stood in the middle of the open field. *What the...?* As she contemplated what had gone wrong, Wendy heard a loud fluttering sound nearby and turned in time to see a startled bird fly away. But when she glanced up into the sky, she smiled. The sun was a perfectly round yellow sphere.

THE ACTRESS

"Not bad," Mallory Sterling murmured when she unlocked the door and surveyed the cabin. As promised, it was fully furnished and the living room looked cozy with a fluffy white rug in front of the stone fireplace.

Wheeling her suitcases inside, Mallory quickly toured the rest of her temporary home. The kitchen had a stove, fridge, dishwasher, and small wooden table with four chairs. Opening the cabinets, she found the necessary plates and pots. Then she fingered the forks in the silverware drawer, tracing their simple design. *Not what I'd choose.*

But that didn't matter. She needed a hideaway, a place where no one could find her—and this little cabin in the woods was perfect. It was isolated, so remote that it didn't have cell service.

She'd gone to the realtor disguised as a blonde divorcée fleeing her obsessive ex-husband. It was an easy role—Gena Whittaker in *Woman on the Run*—a movie she'd starred in twenty years ago. *Had it really been that long?*

Continuing into the bedroom, Mallory sat on the queen-sized bed. The cabin was exactly as described: small but comfy and most importantly, far from Hollywood. Nobody would think to look for her here. It wasn't a vacation home for a glamorous movie star.

Resting her head on the pillow, Mallory closed her eyes as she remembered.

————

Her agent had phoned about the part a week ago. "It's a Dom de Winter movie so it's sure to be a smash," Nita gushed. "And he specifically asked for you."

"Dom called?"

"Not exactly."

"Who called?"

"Eddie, Dom's number one guy. He texted me this morning."

When Mallory went to see the famous producer/director the next day, things had immediately gone wrong. First, she'd been forced to wait nearly twenty minutes until a young girl in obscenely short shorts escorted her into the mogul's majestic office.

"Mallory!" Dom shouted from his throne behind an enormous glass desk. "Thank you for coming." His chubby cheeks widened as he beamed at her.

"Good morning, Dom," she replied, forcing a smile as she sat opposite.

"I've got a terrific part for you. It's a World War Two love story."

"Wonderful! I adore period romances. Who's the male lead?"

"Nigel Bronson. He's just about signed."

Mallory frowned. Nigel was a noted British actor, but... "Isn't he a bit young?" she asked.

"Not at all. He'll be perfect with Daria."

"Daria Fowler?"

"Yes. She's already signed for the lead."

"The lead?"

"Of course. That's why I'm so glad you're here. You'll be terrific as Daria's mother."

"Her mother?" Mallory knew she was babbling, simply repeating Dom's words, but she couldn't help herself. The shock was overwhelming. "You want me to play Daria's mother?"

"It's a wonderful, juicy role. You're the strong woman—a mother who's come to England with her daughter to defeat the Nazis and then Daria meets Nigel, the fighter pilot..."

"I always play the lead," Mallory interrupted, speaking softly.

Dom leaned across his desk and shook his head. "Mallory, sweetheart, you're much too old for the lead in this movie. The girl is supposed to be in her twenties."

Mallory jumped up. "Then make the lead older. She doesn't have to be so goddamn young."

"I'm sorry. The leads are set. Do you want the role of Mrs. Stetson?"

Mallory didn't answer. Instead, she walked out of Dom's office, slamming the door.

––––––

Still fuming at the memory, Mallory rose from the bed and stepped to the window. The view was beautiful: a picturesque little pond surrounded by trees and bushes, part of the cabin's five-acre property. Opening the sliding-glass door, she walked to the pond to examine it more closely.

The small oval body of water was even lovelier up close—crystal-clear and shallow. When she stared at the slight ripples, Mallory saw a few tiny fish and scattered pebbles on the bottom. The surface was free of vegetation—no lilies or algae.

Bending down, she touched the water. It felt comfortably warm. Glad she had packed bathing suits, she returned to the cabin to change.

––––––

Mallory stuck one pedicured big toe into the pond and wiggled the gold-polished nail until she created a small eddy. Then she lowered her body into the little pool and stood on the pebbled floor.

Since the water only reached her waist, she slid under to submerge her shoulders. It felt so good and relaxing that she cupped some water and gently wet her face.

Leaning against the edge, Mallory closed her eyes and considered her options. She needed to sort through the possibilities—maybe write down her thoughts each day. *A diary?*

After applying more clean water to her face, she smiled. Renting the cabin for a week had been a wonderful idea. *I'll figure it out...I know I will.*

––––––

Wednesday, Day 2

I never thought I'd enjoy the quiet life, but I'm loving it here. The only sounds are birdcalls and the occasional pattering of squirrel feet. There are no distractions so I have lots of time to think.

What's my next move? If I refuse to take "old" parts, am I finished? Do I leave Hollywood—and if so, where do I go? Certainly not to New York. I'm sure Billy doesn't want me there anyway. He doesn't need his mother, not when he's got his boyfriend—Butch, I think. What a perfect name!

I took another dip in the pond this afternoon. The water is so clear that I ducked my face under, opened my eyes, and stared at the little fish. It's delightfully relaxing! It must be my imagination, but I thought my arms and hands looked smoother after I dried myself. I'm going into the pond every day—maybe twice a day.

––––––

Thursday, Day 3

Something strange is going on here. This morning I looked at myself in the bathroom mirror and the fine lines under my eyes have disappeared. They really are gone—and I'm sure it's not my imagination. My arms and legs and the rest of my body look much better too.

It has to be the pond. There's something in this water that's tightening my skin and making me look younger, like a fountain of youth.

I'm definitely going into the pond twice today—and I'll dip my head under too. I hope it happens again. Fingers are crossed!

––––––

Friday, Day 4

It's not my imagination. The water in this pond is taking years off my body. Who needs plastic surgery when you can just immerse yourself in this clear pool and watch your skin tighten?

I spent a lot of time today evaluating myself in the mirror. (No nasty comments, please. There's nothing else to do here anyway.) I'm convinced I already look more than ten years younger.

With another three days here—and six more dips in the magical pond—I should knock off another fifteen years. That ought to make me young enough to get any part I want. I can even play the ingénue. The hell with Dom de Winter's goddamn war movie! He—and everyone else—will be begging me to sign.

———

Saturday, Day 5

After today's double dip in the pond, I look at least fifteen years younger. Now I just have to figure out how to explain my new youthful appearance. Obviously I can't tell the truth.

Probably the best story should involve some kind of fantastic new skin treatment. I can say I found a fabulous doctor who's devised an instant method of tightening skin.

Of course everyone will want to know the doctor's name so I'll claim I've been sworn to secrecy because the technique is new and experimental. I'll add that the FDA hasn't approved the treatment yet.

I think this is the best option, but I still have two more days to work on my story—and to lose even more years.

———

Sunday, Day 6

Another two dips into the Pond of Youth, another five years off my appearance. If I keep this up and stay another week, I'll be a child again.

Do I want to relive the bad old days of drunken daddy fighting with angry mommy? They're dead so maybe this time I could get myself adopted by better parents, especially if I played the role of sweet and vulnerable little Mallory...

No, forget that idea. I just want to be a young actress again—and that will happen very soon. After one more day here, I'll return to Hollywood and shock them all.

I can't wait!

———

Monday, Day 7

Since today was my last day, I was tempted to go into the pond three times, just to take off a few more years. But why push it? I look fantastic—younger than that lightweight, Daria Fowler. She can have the lead in Dom de Winter's war movie because I can star in any movie I want. I'm young, I'm beautiful, and unlike Daria, I'm a terrific actress.

I've packed everything and tomorrow morning I'm leaving this glorious little cabin with its magical pond. To explain my transformation, I'm going with the experimental drug story because it allows me to keep the doctor's name and the treatment secret. Even if nobody believes it, who cares? No one will know what really happened and I'm certainly not telling.

The triumphant return of Mallory Sterling! Look out Hollywood, here I come!

———

At nine o'clock Tuesday morning, Mallory locked the cabin and stepped into her rental car. On the back seat were six bottles filled with pond water—for "touch-up" purposes.

Halfway through the three-hour drive, she pulled into a small diner for a break and to call Nita with her exciting news. Opening the rear door to retrieve her handbag, Mallory noticed the water bottles had fallen to the floor. When she picked them up, she discovered all the bottles were empty.

"I guess magic water doesn't like to travel," she murmured before taking out her phone to call Nita. "I can't wait to see you," Mallory said when her agent answered.

"So you feel better after your little vacation?"

"Oh, yes."

"Are you reconsidering the role in Dom's movie? His office called again because, even though you walked out in a huff, he really wants you."

Mallory laughed. "No way! Wait till you see me and you'll know why I can't play Daria's mother."

"Really? Did you have plastic surgery? You told me you'd never let anyone mess with your face."

"This is different."

"Great. Call me when you get home."

Mallory tossed the phone into her bag, entered the diner, and continued to the rest room. As she washed her hands, Mallory peered into the small mirror above the sink to admire herself.

"No!" she shrieked. The face staring back at her was no longer youthful. It was Mallory's face, but the masses of deep wrinkles made her appear at least twenty years older than she had looked a week earlier.

"I told Nita the truth," Mallory whispered as tears streamed down her heavily lined face. "I can't play Daria's mother. I'd have to be her grandmother."

THE GIRL IN APARTMENT 5C

I thought about the girl all the time, even though she had no idea who I was. And if she knew me, she wouldn't have cared. The girl in apartment 5C was way out of my league—tall and gorgeous with glossy black hair, pearly skin, and luminous dark eyes. Me? I'm short, pudgy, and wear glasses—the classic example of a geek.

But I'm not a stalker. Yes, I followed the girl to her apartment once just to find out her name because it wasn't on the mailbox in the lobby. When her name wasn't on the door either, I chose one for her—Penelope—because that sounded elegant and I couldn't imagine her having an ordinary name like Mary or Helen.

Every weekday morning at eight o'clock, Penelope left the building, heading for work, always looking perfect in her black, navy, or gray pantsuit. Since she carried a small attaché case, I figured she was a corporate lawyer or bank officer, although she was pretty enough to be an actress or model.

Since my job has flexible hours—I service computers for three companies—I followed Penelope's daily exits from my first-floor window that faced the street, waiting till she floated out of sight to begin my workday.

———

But one Monday morning, everything changed. Like usual, I watched Penelope leave the building, but the sight of her nearly made me drop my coffee mug.

She looked awful—well, not really awful (she could never look awful)—but awful for Penelope. Her hair was messy, her suit was crumpled, and strangest of all, she wore two different color shoes. One was black and the other was dark blue.

Without thinking, I ran out of my apartment and onto the sidewalk yelling, "Miss! Miss!"

She turned and stared at me with bloodshot eyes. "What's wrong?"

"Your shoes," I said, pointing to the mismatched pair.

"Oh, no!" she cried, tears streaming down her pale cheeks.

I felt horrible. "I'm so sorry to upset you," I stammered, turning to leave.

"No! Don't go!" She grabbed my arm and pulled me back.

"Do you need help with something?" I whispered.

She nodded.

"Please tell me. What can I do?"

Still clutching my arm, the girl pushed me toward the building entrance. "My apartment," she mumbled. "There's a monster inside."

———

We rode the elevator to the fifth floor in silence, Penelope no longer holding onto my arm. When she opened her handbag and took out her house key, her hand shook so much that she was unable to insert it into the lock.

"Let me," I said, feeling like a modern-day Sir Galahad as I opened the door.

But Penelope stood motionless at the entrance to Apartment 5C. "I can't go in there," she whispered.

"Because of the monster?" I asked.

She nodded.

"Should I go in first?"

She grabbed my arm. "No!"

"Then what should we do?"

"I don't know." She burst into tears.

"Maybe you should tell me more about the monster," I suggested. "My apartment's on the first floor. If it's okay with you, we can talk there."

Penelope nodded again. It wasn't exactly romantic, but a gorgeous girl had agreed to come with me to my apartment.

———

"It started Saturday night," the girl began as she sat in my tiny kitchen, drinking coffee. "After Freddy left, I heard sounds."

Freddy? I didn't question the name, but of course she had a boyfriend. "What kind of sounds?" I asked.

"Just little noises at first, like an animal was crawling around."

"Like a mouse?"

She nodded. "Yes, and that was scary enough. I turned on the lights and looked everywhere, but couldn't find anything."

"So what did you do then?"

"I tried to go back to sleep, figuring it was probably nothing—or maybe some creature outside—but the noises didn't stop and I hardly slept."

She did have little bags under her lovely dark brown eyes. *Poor Penelope.* "Did the noises stop in the morning?" I asked.

"I think so. At least I didn't hear anything so I tried to forget about it Sunday, but..."

"You heard noises again last night?"

"Yes. But these sounds were different, much louder, like a big animal—not a mouse—was in the apartment. And when I got out of bed and tiptoed to the door, I saw a shadow in the living room."

"Really?"

"Uh huh. A big thing with spikes on its body was crawling around near the window so I locked the bedroom door and shoved a chair against it. Then I hid under my bed all night."

"Why didn't you call the police?"

"I was afraid if I made any noise the monster would hear it."

"What about this morning? Was the monster gone?"

"I don't know for sure. I got out of the apartment as fast as possible. I wasn't sure what to do. I thought about going to the police, but..."

I looked at her, puzzled.

She shrugged. "This whole story sounds kind of crazy. Who has a monster in their apartment?"

"Why didn't you call someone else then—Freddy?"

"Not him," she said, dismissively.

I suppressed a cheer. "Your family?"

"I'm from Minnesota. I don't have any relatives here."

I smiled at her. "If it's okay with you, I'd like to check your apartment—maybe find and destroy the monster." I wasn't being especially brave. I had an idea about what was going on.

She studied my face. "You believe me?"

I nodded.

"I'm not sure if it's there now. It comes out at night."

"You can stay here meanwhile," I offered. "I'm an IT guy, so I work at home a lot."

"Work!" Penelope looked at her watch. "I have to make a call." After yanking her phone from her handbag, she punched in a number. "Hi," she said. "This is Helen Goodwin. I'm sorry, but I woke up with a terrible headache so I won't be in today."

Penelope's name was Helen. Go figure.

I accompanied Helen to her apartment because she was afraid to be there by herself, even in daytime. Then I sat on her bed while she hurriedly shoved some clothes in a large duffel bag and exchanged her blue and black shoes for sneakers.

"Umm." She glanced at me, looking a little embarrassed.

"Yes?"

"Would it be okay if I took a shower at your place?"

"Of course."

"Thanks!" She gave me a huge, beautiful smile. "You're a real sweetheart. What's your name?"

"Stanley...Stanley Horowitz."

"I'm Helen. Pleased to meet you, Stanley." She extended a long slender arm and I shook her hand. "I'm done," she said, zipping the bag. "Let's get out of here."

We took the elevator down to my apartment.

———

After she showered and changed into a Vikings tee shirt and jeans, Helen insisted I do my work. "I don't want to mess up your day," she said, drying her long black hair with my towel. "I'll be okay. I already feel much better so I could just sit here and watch TV." She gave me another beautiful smile.

"I don't have that much work to do today." Not true. One of my clients had a virus I was supposed to fix, but that could wait till tomorrow. "Do you want to go somewhere?"

"Well..." She tilted her lovely wet head, smiling once more. "I ran out of the apartment without eating anything. How about going out for breakfast?"

A date! Okay, maybe the word "date" is a bit strong—but Helen wanted to go to a restaurant with me. We would be together in a public place and people would see us. At least I hoped they would. Maybe I could take a selfie with her so I'd have proof.

"Stanley?"

"Yes!" I shouted. "Let's have breakfast." I had already eaten, but so what?

———

We walked three blocks to the Olympic Diner and sat in a booth. I was disappointed the restaurant was only half full, but it was Monday morning and most people were at work. Not me, though. I was on a date with Helen, who was devouring her ham omelet like she hadn't eaten in a week.

"This is yummy," she said, lowering her fork for a second. "Great food."

"You've never been to the Olympic?"

She shook her head.

"I eat here a lot," I said. Spiro and his wife, Athena, were super nice people. When I walked in with my date, Spiro had given me a thumbs up.

I sat opposite Helen, ignoring the muffin on my plate, intent on learning more about my gorgeous neighbor. "So what kind of work do you do?" I asked.

"I'm in Sales," she said between bites of home fries.

"That sounds exciting. What do you sell?"

"Cars."

Helen sold cars? I never saw anyone like her when I bought my Civic.

"What's wrong?" she asked.

"Nothing." I guess I looked surprised. "I just thought you had a different kind of job."

"Like what?"

I shrugged. "Maybe a banker or a model."

She chuckled. "I'm not good with math—and I'm a total klutz. I would fall off a runway."

"Really?"

"Yup. You're a nice guy, Stanley. I'm so glad I met you." As she patted my arm, her face became serious. "But I still have to deal with the monster in my apartment."

"I'm sure I can help you with that tonight."

"I hope so," she said, patting my arm again. "I really hope so."

———

After breakfast, Helen decided to go shopping. "I'm treating this like a vacation day and I'll try to forget about all the bad stuff. I'll be at your place by five at the latest—and I'll bring dinner."

I guess that meant we were on our own for lunch. "Okay," I muttered. "See you then." I forced a smile, trying to hide my disappointment.

But as I headed home, I began feeling better. I'd have time to work on my client's virus—and more importantly, I had a definite dinner date.

———

Helen lowered her fork and sighed. "I guess we have to check my apartment now."

"It'll be all right," I said, mumbling my reassurance as I stuffed one last piece of General Tso's chicken into my mouth. Helen's takeout from a Chinese restaurant I'd never tried, was delicious.

During dinner, she'd been quieter than before, I'm sure because she was nervous about the monster. She certainly wasn't nervous about me.

We took the elevator to Apartment 5C and this time, although her hand shook slightly, Helen managed to unlock the door. "Can I wait outside?" she whispered.

"Sure." I hoped I sounded brave as I boldly entered the apartment, along with two shopping bags filled with Helen's purchases. "Where's your computer?" I asked.

"Why?"

"I think the monster's there."

"Inside the computer?"

"Kind of...Where is it?"

"Still in my briefcase. I left it in the bedroom when I came back with you this morning."

I might have been able to slay the monster earlier, but then I would've missed all this additional time with Helen. Also, I wanted to see its nighttime performance.

"What are you doing?" Helen called from the apartment's entrance.

"Waiting for the monster to show up."

"Why?"

"So I'll know how to kill it."

Helen didn't answer right away. "You're confusing me," she finally said.

"I'll explain everything aft..." I stopped talking when I heard the monster.

———

The noises started slowly with a few low grunts and groans.

"Do you hear that?" Helen called.

"Yes."

"Aren't you scared?"

"No." It was easy to be brave knowing the monster was phony.

"Do you see it?"

"Not yet." I waited patiently in the living room.

As the noises got louder, I turned on a lamp. Just as I did, a shadow, much like Helen described, appeared under the window. It was a big round thing with pointed spikes, maybe the size of a beach ball.

The creature seemed to open its mouth just as a loud "roar" sounded. Very clever indeed—and scary—if you didn't know it was fake. Ignoring the beastly shadow and the noises, I walked into Helen's bedroom, grabbed the attaché case, and left the apartment.

"What happened just now?" Helen asked as I closed the front door.

"I saw the monster."

"And you weren't scared?"

At this point, I had to tell her the truth. "It's all a trick," I said. "Somebody put this monster in your laptop and I'm going to remove it." Even if I wasn't a brave knight, I could still save the damsel in distress.

Helen gave me a quick kiss on the cheek and I felt like a hero.

———

Back in my apartment, I fiddled with her laptop, looking for the rogue entity. "Who else had access to your computer?" I asked, playing detective.

She shrugged. "Anyone, I guess. I take the laptop to work because I use it there sometimes. I like it better than the one at the dealership."

"Did you have a fight with a coworker or a friend?"

"No."

"What about that guy, Freddy?"

"What about him?"

"You mentioned that he was in your apartment Saturday night."

She hesitated before speaking. "He's not important and he never was anywhere near my laptop."

Not important. I liked that. And he hadn't been in her bedroom. I liked that too. I checked the programs again—and *voila!* There it was.

"I found it," I announced, trying not to sound overly triumphant.

"Really?" Helen stood next to me as I highlighted the culprit.

"When I get rid of this piece of malware, your monster will disappear forever," I said as I clicked "Delete."

"You're the best, Stanley," Helen said, honoring me with a second soft kiss on the cheek.

———

We returned to Helen's apartment. "Everything will be fine now," I promised.

Helen studied my face. "I'm sure you're right," she said. "But can I ask you a favor?"

"Sure, anything."

"I don't want to be alone tonight so could you stay here with me?"

A beautiful girl asking me to spend the night with her? "Of course," I said.

We went back to my place for my pajamas and toothbrush and again took the elevator to the fifth floor. When Helen unlocked her door and turned on the lights, there were no noises, no shadows—no monsters.

"See? It's okay now," I said.

"I know, but..." She frowned, scanning the living room.

"What's wrong?"

"I'm not sure." Her frown morphed into a smile. "It's probably nothing, just some leftover nerves." She turned on the TV to Netflix. "Let's watch a movie. Pick one."

I chose *The Proposal* because it was a comedy. Helen needed a few laughs and I liked the title. Maybe it would get Helen into a romantic mood. I was already there.

We watched the movie, laughed a bit, but Helen yawned throughout. "I'm sorry," she apologized when it ended. "I'm so tired from not sleeping at all last night. I've got to go to bed."

"I understand," I said, trying to hide my disappointment at our date ending so soon.

"Will you be okay on the couch?"

"I'll be fine," I assured her as I fluffed the pillow and covered myself with the blanket she had given me.

———

A scuffling sound startled me out of a deep sleep. Sitting up in the dark room, I listened carefully but didn't hear anything else. Figuring it must have been Helen moving around in the bedroom, I lay down again and closed my eyes.

"Grrr..."

When I heard the low growling noise, I turned on the lamp next to the couch, but didn't see anything. I sat quietly, waiting for another growl, which never came. After several minutes of silence, I switched off the light.

Was it my imagination? I didn't think so, but maybe the sound came from a dog outside the building. That was the only possibility that made sense.

Footsteps! Something was walking near me in the living room. *Helen?* Opening my eyes, I tilted my head towards the new sound. *Nothing.*

Feeling foolish, I sat up. There was no monster. It was just a clever bit of malware—and I had deleted it. But something was making strange noises.

I was now fully awake and there was no way I could go back to sleep.

———

In the dark living room, I sat motionless on the couch, waiting for the next sound. The only good thing about all this was Helen still seemed to be fast asleep.

Scratching noises. Something was tearing at the carpet by the chair to my left. Did I dare turn on the light and confront the perpetrator?

Taking a deep breath, I grabbed my watch—the only weapon on hand—and switched on the lamp. The scratching sounds immediately stopped and the room was silent again.

Slowly I rose, snatched a pen from the table—a second weapon—and tiptoed towards the green chair. Then, in one quick motion, I flung the chair around and saw—nothing. However, the carpet underneath looked frayed, as if it had been chewed.

No. I shook my head. That was my imagination. It was just a small defect in the rug. Returning to the couch, I sat again, leaving the light on.

––––––

The apartment remained silent and unthreatening with no more creepy sounds or scary moving shadows. When I checked my watch, it was only 2:14. Since I wasn't going back to sleep, I needed to do something productive.

I remembered leaving Helen's laptop on the kitchen table when we returned to her apartment. Tiptoeing as quietly as I could, I reached the kitchen doorway. As I fumbled for the light switch, I heard a new noise—a whimpering sound that seemed to be coming from inside one of the cabinets. I tried to convince myself it was nothing as I turned on the light, grabbed the laptop, and rushed out of the room.

Then I got to work on Helen's computer, searching for a second rogue entity. I'd assumed there was only one, but there had to be another and I had the rest of the night to find it. The apartment was quiet again—obviously this mythical creature was dormant in the light—so there were no distractions.

I will find the evil monster and slay it, I vowed. After all, I was Helen's gallant knight.

––––––

By the time the sun rose, my eyes were blurry and I hadn't found any other malicious program. I closed both the laptop and my eyes and tried to concentrate. *What am I missing?*

I'd gone through everything and the laptop was clean. So if a hidden entity wasn't responsible for the monster, it had to be something else, something logical. *A talking animal toy, timed to go on and off at night at set intervals?*

Walking quietly into the kitchen, I slowly opened the cabinet where I'd heard the whimpering sound. After removing a bunch of pots and pans, I found—nothing.

"What are you doing?"

I glanced from the pots on the floor to Helen's lovely face, which looked sleepy, but much better than yesterday. "I thought I might make us some breakfast," I lied, scooping up a frying pan.

"Oh, that's so sweet," she said, wrapping the blue terrycloth robe tightly around her perfect waist. "Let me help you. We can have breakfast together before I go to work."

———

So I had a second breakfast with Helen. I was enjoying these food dates immensely.

"How was everything last night?" she asked as she took a bite of scrambled eggs.

"Fine."

"That's great to hear. I slept wonderfully." She gave me a great big smile. "I felt so safe knowing you were in the next room."

I tried to return her smile.

"I'd love to stay and talk some more," Helen said, sipping coffee as she stood. "But I have to get ready. After missing work yesterday, I want to get in early."

"Would you like me to wait here?"

She shook her head. "Thanks to you, I should be okay now."

No, you shouldn't. But I didn't say that.

———

I needed a reason to return to Helen's apartment. However, I was too exhausted to do any constructive thinking so I crawled into my bed and immediately fell asleep.

When I woke up, it was nearly two o'clock. After showering, dressing, and eating lunch in record time, I sat by the window to figure out how I could spend the night at Helen's place without frightening her.

Since everything I thought of had negatives, I decided to go with a half-truth. Helen had given me her cell number so, before she left work, I called her.

"Hi, it's Stanley," I began.

"Is everything okay?"

"Yes, but I still have a concern."

"Really? You said there's no more monster."

"Umm, that's right. But I think there could be a little trace left."

"In my laptop?"

"Probably." Another lie. Her laptop was fine.

"What do you want me to do?"

"I'd like to stay at your apartment again tonight and check your laptop—just to make sure."

"All right." She didn't sound thrilled, but she didn't sound mad either.

"I'll get dinner for us," I offered.

"Thanks."

I heard a commotion in the background.

"Can't talk. Got to go." Helen ended the call.

———

Our second dinner, this time in Helen's apartment, wasn't as good as the first. My date wasn't her bubbly self, which was understandable since I'd hinted the monster might still be in the apartment. Although Helen replied to everything I said, she didn't smile or talk much.

"So what do we do now?" she asked when we'd finished the pizza.

"If you want, I can go back to my apartment and come back about eight—just before it gets dark."

"No. You can stay."

She didn't sound very inviting. "Is something wrong?" I asked.

Helen sighed. "I don't really understand what's happening. You said you got rid of this monster, but then you called..."

I guess my half-truth idea didn't work. "I'm sorry," I began. "Unfortunately, I don't understand what's happening either. Although I deleted the monster program, last night I saw and heard some strange things again."

"You told me everything was okay. Did you lie to me, Stanley?"

I shrugged. "I didn't want to upset you."

"Oh, you're so sweet." She smiled, walked over, and kissed my cheek. "I'm staying up with you tonight and we'll figure this out together."

———

I went downstairs to get my pajamas and toothbrush. When I returned to Apartment 5C, Helen had removed her makeup and was wearing the blue terrycloth robe. Even with no makeup, she looked stunning.

"Now I want to hear what really happened last night," she said as we sat together on the couch.

I told her about the strange noises and showed her the frayed carpet.

"That could have already been there," she said, pointing to the damaged spot. "I haven't moved this chair in months."

"But I heard animal sounds too. Something's going on here."

"We'll find out what it is," she said, giving me a reassuring pat on the hand.

———

We sat in the dark living room watching CNN. Helen had lowered the volume so we could read the news headlines flashing at the bottom of the screen and still listen for strange noises.

"Do you hear anything?" she asked.

"Not yet."

"When did it start last night?"

"About one-thirty."

Helen yawned. "Then maybe I should go to sleep now and you can wake me as soon as something happens."

"Sure." So much for our date.

Helen retreated to her bedroom and I was alone again. I could barely hear the TV and what I did hear was boring so I leaned against the cushions and closed my eyes.

———

The growls woke me. Annoyed at having fallen asleep when I was supposed to be on guard duty, I leaned forward and squinted in the darkness, searching for the source of the sounds.

They seemed to be coming from behind the closed living room

curtains. Grabbing the carving knife I'd taken from Helen's kitchen drawer, I crept to the window and pushed apart the drapes. Something darted out and ran into the kitchen.

I turned on a lamp and, walking backwards, knocked on the bedroom door.

"Get up," I called, not screaming, but not whispering either. After all, Helen wanted to be included.

"What time is it?" she muttered.

"I don't know, but something's in your kitchen. Hurry!" Nothing had run out so the growling creature was still in there.

Helen joined me, tying her robe as she closed the door behind her. "Is it the monster?"

"Maybe."

"What are we going to do?"

Good question. "For a start, we're turning on the kitchen light. Then we'll find whatever's in there."

———

With the kitchen light on, Helen stood behind me holding the knife as I flung open each cabinet and backed away, expecting some kind of creature to pop out.

"How big was it?" Helen asked after we'd searched every bottom cabinet and uncovered nothing but pots, pans, and ordinary kitchen supplies.

"About the size of a raccoon."

"Then it can't be a mouse."

"No. Maybe a rat on steroids." But it didn't have a long tail and wasn't shaped like a rodent.

"Did it have spikes?"

"I'm not sure," I said. "It moved too fast." I glanced at the upper cabinets. "I'll start with the ones above the stove. Here goes."

But we found only dishes and food. All that was left were three high cabinets. "I'll need a stepladder to reach those," I said.

"I'll get it," Helen said. As soon as she left the kitchen, I heard her scream.

———

A trembling Helen stood in the entrance to the living room.

"What happened?" I asked.

She ran to me, burying her head in my shoulders as I put my arms around her. It felt so good to hold her that I almost forgot about our problem.

"The monster..." Helen reminded me, pointing with a shaky finger. "It ran right past me into the bedroom."

Reluctantly, I let go of her and picked up the carving knife she'd dropped. "Did you see what it was?"

She shook her head.

"But wasn't the light on here?"

"Yes." Helen turned to me. "I thought the monster only came out in the dark."

"Until now," I said.

"What should we do?"

"Go into your bedroom." I didn't want to do that, but we couldn't leave whatever it was in there.

"Maybe we should call the police," Helen suggested.

"Maybe they'll think we're crazy."

"But both of us saw it."

"Yeah, two crazy people. And what if the police don't find anything? Whatever it is, it keeps evading us."

"You're right," Helen agreed. "We have to do this ourselves—together."

I liked the "together" part. But that's the only thing I liked.

———

With me holding the carving knife and Helen following with a steak knife, we tiptoed to her bedroom. I switched on the light and Helen shut the door behind us. Although we were scared of what was in here, we were more scared of letting it escape again.

"Where is it?" Helen whispered.

"I don't know."

We stood motionless in front of the door waiting for a growl or some sign from the creature, but the room remained silent.

"I'll search," I said softly. "You wait here."

Helen nodded and moved her knife to a ready-to-stab position, although I doubted she'd ever use it.

Crawling to the bed, I looked underneath. But it was empty. Then, slowly, I opened her dresser drawers, one by one. Although they made slight creaking noises, nothing jumped out.

Working my way around the room, I opened the night table drawer, even though it was too small for the creature we'd seen to fit inside. That drawer was stuffed with papers, nothing else.

When I peeked behind the headboard, I saw dust, but no monster. Glancing at Helen, I shrugged.

She pointed to the two curtained windows. I nodded and quickly pushed apart the first set of drapes. Nothing.

The second curtain billowed slightly. "Did you leave the window open?" I whispered.

Helen shook her head.

When I parted the curtains, the window was wide open. Outside, a street lamp provided just enough light for me to see something scamper into the dark street. "It's gone," I said, shutting the window.

———

Helen sat on her living room sofa, holding her head in her hands. "I can't live like this," she moaned.

"Maybe you should move out?" I suggested.

"And go where?"

I shrugged and spoke softly. "You can stay in my apartment until we find a way to get rid of the monster."

"Really?" She lifted her head and stared at my face. "You'd do that for me?"

"Of course." It would be for me too. But I didn't say that.

Helen spread her arms wide and yawned. "Can we go to your apartment now. I'm so tired."

"Sure."

And that's how I got a beautiful girl to spend the night with me. Well, sort of. She slept in my bed and I slept on the couch.

———

Helen stayed with me the rest of that week. She packed her clothes and other things she needed and we brought them to my apartment.

Each night, we returned to Apartment 5C to look for the monster. Several times, we heard growls and grunts or saw mysterious shadows, but we didn't find the creature.

After that week, Helen continued to share my apartment and gradually everything but her furniture and kitchen utensils ended up downstairs too. I was in heaven with my new roommate, but I didn't know how she felt.

———

"Stanley," Helen said about a month later during breakfast. "Since I'm living here, I want to help pay the rent."

"But you're still paying for Apartment 5C," I pointed out.

"I've been thinking about that."

"Oh?"

She lowered the coffee mug and shook her beautiful head. "I'm giving up 5C because I'm never living there again."

"I can certainly understand that."

Helen tilted her head and studied my face. "Do you like me?" she whispered.

"Like you? Of course I like you...I more than like you, I love..." I stopped talking because I was babbling.

"You've never kissed me."

"You want me to kiss you?"

Helen smiled and nodded.

So I kissed her and then I more than kissed her. And then...well, I'll just say that I moved back into my bedroom and Helen and I became more than roommates.

All this happened six months ago. And last week, Helen Goodwin became Mrs. Stanley Horowitz. I can hardly believe my luck.

The monster? We never found it, but we keep tabs on Apartment 5C and something's still going on there. Tenants who move in never stay longer than a week.

And even if I found the creature, I wouldn't hurt it. I owe that monster a huge "thank you."

THE ISLAND

What's burning?

Katy McWilliams smelled the smoke before opening her eyes and when she did, she immediately closed them, not wanting to remember. She had been on a sightseeing trip with three other tourists, snapping aerial photos of a small island when something went terribly wrong.

"Mayday!" the pilot had shouted into the radio while fumbling desperately with the controls. "We're going down!"

As the plane nosedived, Katy had unsnapped her seatbelt. *Why?* She had no clue. But that move had saved her life, throwing her into a bed of thick grass while the others...

Opening her eyes again, Katy stared at the burning metal coffin and said a silent prayer for the passengers and pilot. Then she rose, swaying unsteadily until a wave of dizziness forced her down.

Since she was sitting, Katy did a quick self-exam, grateful that her job as a medical assistant gave her a decent knowledge of traumatic injuries. She flexed her arms and legs and, miraculously, nothing seemed to be broken, although her right shoulder felt sore.

As she slid backwards, trying to further distance herself from the fiery wreckage, Katy realized the flames had lessened, meaning she'd probably been unconscious for a while. Checking her wrist, she discovered the shattered watch no longer worked. *Phone?* Lost onboard the doomed plane.

That's when the realization hit Katy: She was trapped on the island.

———

Maybe I'm not alone.

The idea was comforting. The island had seemed tiny from the sky, but perhaps it was larger than she'd thought. Willing herself to stand, Katy walked slowly toward the sounds of waves lapping against the shore.

Her head felt better, lessening the possibility of a concussion, and the hike was short. When she reached the ocean, Katy continued to explore the periphery, which was pebbly and uninteresting until...

She gasped at the unexpected sight. A small motorboat lay halfway up the rocky beach.

"Hello!" she shouted, walking faster. "Is anyone here?"

A bird squawked in response. Then silence.

But when Katy got close enough to examine the vessel, she dropped to her knees and wept. The craft was nothing but a rotted shell filled with debris and crawling insects.

The boat's owner? What happened to him?

———

Katy finished circling the shoreline without finding anything else of note. Unfortunately, the island was as small as she had thought. After using a stick to carve "HELP" on the pebbly beach—large enough, she hoped, to be seen by a search plane—Katy headed inland.

She needed to get home. The weeklong vacation had been a luxury—an expensive one. In addition to the trip, she'd doubled Anna's salary to care full-time for her father, who suffered from dementia. *If I'm not back...*

Katy shook her head, willing herself to focus on exploring the interior of the island. Avoiding several jutting rocks, she entered a woodsy area with a few scraggly trees and numerous berry bushes.

Plucking a purple berry, she tossed it into her mouth. The fruit was ripe and sweet. *At least I won't starve.*

She grabbed a handful of berries, munching them as she reached a grassy clearing. "Wow!" she murmured, staring at the colorful meadow filled with blue, red, yellow, and orange wildflowers. *Like a movie scene.*

As she traipsed through the flower-laden field, Katy saw a variety of flying insects and clusters of long brown worms, which she tried to avoid trampling. Noticing something white glistening in the grass, she picked it up.

"Yucch!" Katy muttered, quickly dropping the object—a large bone. When she moved forward, she saw several more bones, and then a skull—definitely from a human.

Katy no longer had any desire to stroll through the beautiful meadow. She took a step backwards, anxious to leave.

———

Feeling a tug on her left leg, Katy glanced down. One of the long brown worms had wrapped itself tightly around her ankle and now slithered up her jeans. Using both hands, she yanked it off.

As she ran towards the trees, a second worm crawled over her sneaker and onto her right leg. Again she stopped to wrench it off. But while Katy worked at removing that worm, a third one inched up her left leg—followed by another and another until an army of worms occupied her body. The invaders marched up her torso, some camping on her face and head.

"Help!" Katy yelled as she struggled to yank the worms from her eyes and mouth. But as soon as she succeeded in pulling one worm off, many reinforcements took its place.

"Please someone help me!" Katy yelled again as her knees, bound together by bands of elongated worms, buckled, and she collapsed into the flowery meadow, her body now covered entirely with worms.

"Help," she whispered from the ground, arms flailing at the wriggling creatures as one of them squeezed into her mouth and others immediately followed, preventing her from saying anything else. Worms continued to enter her mouth or wind themselves tightly around her head and the rest of her torso until Katy's arms fell slack and she stopped thrashing.

The grassy field was again quiet. It still boasted blue, yellow, orange, and red wildflowers, but now it featured a new color: a five-foot slithery mound of brown.

VISIONARY GIRL

"The lenses in these glasses are made of a new material," Dr. Halstead told Jayda Johnson as he checked her vision. "You're the first to try them."

Jayda peered at the eye chart through the frames she'd just purchased. "They feel the same and my vision's the same too. What's so different?"

The optometrist shrugged. "It's a special kind of plastic that's supposed to be unscratchable, unbreakable—an overall better quality lens." He walked her to the counter and smiled. "Please let me know what you think of them."

"Sure," Jayda said as she left the office.

————

Jayda promptly forgot about the glasses. She spent the rest of Saturday running errands and preparing for her date with Travis, a guy she'd met on Match.com. She'd been out with him once and sort of liked him.

"So what did you do today?" Travis asked as they dined at L'Escargot, a fancy downtown restaurant.

"Nothing much. The highlight was getting these glasses." She fingered the silver frames.

"Nice," Travis said, admiring her. "Great contrast with your dark skin."

As Jayda continued to look at her date, his face became blurry and she no longer saw him seated opposite her in the restaurant. Instead, he was riding a blue bicycle on a suburban street and as she watched, the bike crashed into a tree.

She closed her eyes, blinked, and again looked at Travis, now clearly in focus.

"Is something wrong?" he asked.

"For a moment, I thought I saw..." Jayda began. "Do you ride a blue bike?"

"Yes. Why?"

"I'm not sure. Did you ever have an accident—like crash the bike into a tree?"

"No." Travis stared at her.

"I'm sorry." Jayda shook her head. "I guess I must be tired."

———

Jayda had a quiet Sunday morning. She jogged around her neighborhood—a mile-long sprint she tried to do once each weekend. Then, as she stepped out of the shower, her cellphone rang. Recognizing Travis' number, Jayda wrapped herself in the towel and took the call.

"What you said last night—about me on the bike," Travis said breathlessly, without even a "hello."

"I asked if you'd ever crashed into a tree."

"It happened just now—exactly like you described. A dog shot out in front of me and when I swerved to avoid it, my bike smashed into a big tree."

For a long moment, Jayda didn't speak. "Are you hurt?" she finally asked.

"Not really. I've got some scrapes and cuts and the bike's a mess, but I'll be okay. How did you know this would happen?"

"I didn't know. I just saw..." Jayda didn't finish her sentence because she wasn't sure what she'd seen. "I'm glad you're all right," she said instead.

Jayda tried to relax and enjoy the rest of Sunday, but her mind kept returning to Travis' accident. *How did I see that?* She didn't understand her strange vision.

On Monday, Jayda went to work. As a customer rep for Heilbruner's Insurance, she sat in her cubicle and fielded phone calls with two other employees. She didn't like the job, but she needed the money and the position she really wanted—art historian—was hard to find. Although she continued to network and email resumés, the results were disappointing. Not one interview.

For Jayda, the best thing about Heilbruner's was lunch with her coworker, Daphne, an aspiring actress.

"So I've got an audition tonight for a TV commercial," Daphne said as they sat in their usual back booth in Finn's Coffee Shop. "It's big bucks because it's for a Ford dealer. I'm driving their new sports car and loving the ride."

"Great," Jayda said, taking a bite of her chicken wrap. "Hope you get it."

"Oh, I will." Daphne nodded, bright red hair bouncing around her face. "They've already guaranteed me the job."

"Really?" Jayda looked up at Daphne and saw the redhead—not in the restaurant—but on a stage in a small auditorium, holding a sheet of paper.

As Jayda watched, Daphne walked off the stage and handed the paper to a middle-aged man in the first row of the audience, who shook his head and said something to her. Although Jayda couldn't hear him, she saw the man's lips form the words, "I'm sorry."

"Hey, Jayda, are you okay?"

Jayda blinked and Daphne again sat opposite her in the booth, a concerned expression on her face. "Yes, I'm fine."

"You had this weird look, like you were someplace else."

"That audition you mentioned, the one for the TV commercial, maybe you shouldn't go."

"Why?"

"You might not get the job."

"How can you say that? The guy in charge promised me I'd get it."

Jayda shrugged. "Just a feeling."

———

At nine o'clock that evening, Jayda's doorbell rang. Peeking through the keyhole, she saw Daphne.

"How did you know?" the teary-eyed redhead asked as she brushed past Jayda and sat on the couch.

"The commercial?" Jayda asked, pressing "Mute" on the remote.

Daphne nodded. "I didn't get the job. They went with a guy instead of a girl because Ford decided it was more of a man's car. Mr. Caldwell said he loved me as the driver, but his hands were tied." She stared at Jayda. "But you couldn't have known all that."

"I didn't."

"You told me you had a feeling."

"It's more than that." Jayda took off her glasses and gave them to Daphne. "I got these on Saturday and since then I've gotten weird visions. When I look at people, I see things before they happen. I saw Travis have a bike accident and at lunch, I saw a man at your audition shake his head and tell you, 'I'm sorry.'"

"Glasses?" Daphne fingered the silver frames.

"It's the lenses. The optometrist told me they're some kind of new plastic."

"That's nuts."

"I know."

"Still..." Daphne turned the glasses around in her hands. "Let me put them on and look at you. Maybe I'll see something." She slid the eyeglasses over her head and stared at Jayda. "I can't see a damn thing. Everything's blurry."

"Of course it is," Jayda said, chuckling as she reclaimed her glasses. "They're prescription and you're not nearsighted."

———

As Jayda lay in bed, unable to sleep, her thoughts kept going back to the strange glasses. *Return them? Maybe not...*

Wide-awake now, Jayda sat up. Twice she had seen things shortly before they'd happened. If that pattern continued, she could be a real-life super hero—saving people from future accidents or disappointments.

"I can even secretly call myself something clever, like Visionary Girl," she murmured. Smiling at her clever idea, she dropped her head onto the pillow and promptly fell asleep.

———

Jayda decided to put her plan into action immediately. After arriving at Heilbruner's Tuesday morning, she marched into Paulette Morovik's cubicle and wriggled into the chair facing the woman. "So how're you doing this morning?" she asked the fortyish brunette.

"You know exactly how I'm doing," her coworker retorted. "I hate being here and I'd rather be anywhere else."

Paulette was a gourmet cook who yearned to own and operate a restaurant.

"Besides that," Jayda continued, smiling and staring at the woman's flashing brown eyes. "Anything new happening in your life?"

"Why are you looking at me like that, Jayda? What's wrong with you today?" Paulette swiveled her chair so it faced her desk and turned on the computer. "Get out of here and go to work."

———

"So that's what I'm trying to do," Jayda concluded, having explained her superhero theory to Daphne during lunch at Finn's. "But I have to find people who need my help. Obviously, Paulette doesn't."

"Our office's too small," Daphne said. "You've got to go someplace with lots of people."

"Like a park or a mall?"

"Yeah."

"But if I stare at people, they'll think I'm nuts."

"You've got to be subtle—not obviously looking. Like this." Lowering her head, Daphne snuck a quick glance at Jayda.

"You're right." Jayda paused for a moment. "I think I know a way, but I'll need your help. Can you come with me after work?"

"Sure," Daphne said, smiling. "I can't wait to see Visionary Girl in action."

———

Jayda and Daphne again sat at a table, this time eating dinner at the local mall's food court. Each had two slices of pizza and a bottle of water and Jayda held a magazine near her face.

"I'm going to try staring at her," Jayda whispered, nodding towards the skinny woman munching on a sandwich at the table opposite.

"I can't see your subject," Daphne said, "and I don't want to turn around and arouse her suspicion. Tell me if you learn something, oh great Visionary Girl."

Jayda put down the magazine and took a small bite of pizza as she gazed at the woman. "Nothing." She lowered her eyes and the slice. "I thought this part would be easy. It worked so fast with you and Travis."

"I guess not everyone has important stuff happening in their lives so..." Daphne lowered her voice. "An interesting-looking guy just sat down behind you."

"What's interesting about him?"

"I'm not sure, but he's cute and seems kind of sad. Get up casually, sit next to me, and try your magic on him."

———

He is cute. Holding her pizza slice, Jayda focused on the man sitting at the table across from her. Unfortunately, however, the guy remained face down, busily eating his wrap.

"He's not looking up," Jayda whispered.

"He has to look up sometime."

"Not necessarily. I think he's in a hurry so when he finishes his food, he might just leave."

"Keep staring at him."

"I am." Jayda kept her eyes on the man as he continued to concentrate on the wrap. "Told you," she muttered as he jumped up, tossed his tray on top of the trashcan, and left the food court.

"Follow him," Daphne ordered.

"Why? There are plenty of other people here."

"I have a feeling he needs your help."

―――――

"What if he's going to his car?" Jayda asked as she and Daphne stood on the top steps of the down escalator, their quarry about to exit on the ground floor.

"He's not leaving the mall."

"How can you be sure? He ate so quickly that he could be in a hurry to go home."

"No. I have another feeling."

"Maybe you're the real superhero," Jayda said. "Mind-Reading Girl."

"Look!" Daphne shouted, pointing. "He's going into Great Gifts."

When Jayda and Daphne entered the store, their prey was fingering a crystal necklace and frowning.

"See," Daphne whispered. "I told you he's upset about something. Try to stare into his eyes."

"How am I supposed to do that? He's still not looking up."

"He's about to look up. Stand behind me and be ready." Daphne walked over to the man and casually brushed against him. "Excuse me," she said, smiling.

As the man glanced at Daphne, Jayda met his eyes, staring at him through her special lenses. And this time, something happened.

―――――

The stranger's face blurred and when Jayda blinked, the man was sitting on a living room sofa next to an attractive curly-haired brunette. The marble table held an open box with a crystal necklace.

The woman shook her head and started crying. As the man reached for her hand, she brushed it away. Then the brunette picked up the box with the necklace, shoved it into the man's hand, stood, and pointed to the door.

The vision dimmed and Jayda again saw the stranger, still holding the necklace, and looking at her. "Don't buy it," she said.

"What?" he asked.

"I'm sorry. I know this sounds weird, but that necklace..." Jayda pointed to the crystal piece. "She won't take it."

"What are you talking about?"

"The brunette with the curly hair that you're going to give this necklace to—trust me, she won't like it. She'll cry, hand it back to you, and tell you to leave."

"You're crazy," the man said as he scooped up the necklace and headed to the cashier.

———

"That really worked well," Jayda muttered as she watched the man pay for the necklace and leave the store.

"You tried. Let's find someone else."

Jayda and Daphne strolled along the first floor corridor. "This was a bad idea," Jayda said after staring at several shoppers and not seeing anything but their faces. "We should go home."

"No. Give it a little more time. Try this store." Daphne pushed Jayda towards Jeans for Teens. "Maybe you'll have more luck with kids."

Several high-school age girls pawed through a "SALE!" rack at the front of the store. As an African-American teen met Jayda's eyes, things got blurry again.

———

When Jayda's vision cleared, the girl sat in the window seat of a plane, looking at the runway below, surrounded by tiny palm trees. But as Jayda continued to watch, the plane's slow and steady descent became a free-fall, hurtling towards the ground.

"No," Jayda said, shaking her head and closing her eyes.

"What's the matter?" Daphne asked.

Ignoring the question, Jayda opened her eyes and faced the puzzled teen.

"Why are you looking at me like that?" the girl asked. "Do I know you?"

"You don't," Jayda said. "And I apologize for staring, but I saw something just now that concerns you." She took the girl's hand and squeezed it. "This will sound strange, but I need you to believe me."

Jayda, Daphne, and the teen walked out of the store together and sat on a hall bench. "I'm Jayda and this is Daphne," Jayda began.

"What's your name?"

"Tamryn."

"You're going on a trip soon, Tamryn—to a warm place with palm trees."

"Nassau in the Bahamas tomorrow. But how did you know that?"

"I can see things before they happen."

"Huh?"

"It's true," Daphne said. "She saw something yesterday, just before it happened to me."

"On the plane tomorrow," Jayda continued, "you'll sit next to the window, watching as your plane crashes before landing. That's what I just saw about to happen."

"No way." The girl stood and took several steps back, a horrified expression on her face.

"Please listen to me, Tamryn," Jayda begged. "I saw the plane about to crash. You have to call the airline and tell them to check all their planes. Maybe cancel your trip and go another time."

The girl shook her head. "My parents planned this vacation last year. They won't believe your story—and I don't believe it either. Why are you doing this? Do you work for another airline and want to get me to switch to your plane?"

"No, nothing like that. I don't even know what airline you're taking. I'm just trying to save your life and the lives of the other people on that plane."

Shaking her head again, the girl turned and ran towards the other end of the mall.

———

"What now?" Daphne asked.

"We should phone all the airlines going to Nassau tomorrow and find the one Tamryn's booked on," Jayda said, wiping her tear-filled eyes with her hand. "Her name's so unusual that it should be easy to find her plane."

"The airlines won't give us that information—and they'll want to know why we're asking about her. It'll seem suspicious."

"I have to try," Jayda said. "Come on."

"Where are we going?"

"Upstairs. We can't use our cells so I'm hoping this old mall still has a public phone."

On the second floor, outside the rest rooms, they spotted a wall-mounted phone. "Check your phone for airlines flying to the Bahamas tomorrow," Jayda said.

Daphne found seven airlines that had daily flights to Nassau in the Bahamas and Jayda started with American Airlines, the first on the list. "I need to know if a teenage girl named Tamryn is booked for a flight to Nassau in the Bahamas out of New York tomorrow," she began.

"Are you a relative?" the woman on the phone asked.

"Not exactly..."

"Then that's confidential information."

"But it's important."

"Why?"

"She might be in danger."

"How?"

"The plane..."

The woman lowered her voice. "Are you reporting a bomb? Is this girl carrying an explosive on the flight?"

"No, nothing like that."

"Please stay on the line while I..."

Jayda quickly hung up the phone.

———

"Great," Daphne said. "Now Tamryn's a suspected terrorist." Shaking her head, she turned to Jayda. "You're only making it worse."

"What could be worse than a plane crash? I'm trying to save lives."

"But what you're doing isn't working."

"I have another idea. How about contacting the media—TV, radio, newspapers?"

"And tell them what?"

"That a plane to Nassau could be damaged and might crash."

"And just how did you know that? And which plane?" Daphne sighed. "It's not going to work, Jayda. You'll just have the cops looking for you, thinking you did something to damage a plane." She tugged her friend's arm. "Let's get out of the mall before something else bad happens."

———

At Heilbruner's on Wednesday, Jayda had trouble concentrating on work. "I keep checking my phone for a report of a plane crash in the Bahamas," she told Daphne.

"Try not to think about it."

"I hate these lenses," Jayda said, taking off her glasses and rubbing her eyes. "What's the good of being able to see bad things before they happen if I can't do anything to prevent them?"

"I don't know," Daphne said, shaking her head.

When Jayda and Daphne left the office at five o'clock, Jayda still hadn't found any mention of a plane crash.

"Maybe it's a night flight," Daphne suggested.

"Most of today's flights to the Bahamas were in the morning and afternoon," Jayda pointed out. "And the crash I saw was in daylight. But I'll keep checking."

———

At home, Jayda continued to search for information about the crash. When she typed "Bahamas," "Nassau," "plane crash," and the date, she got nothing. But after entering the name of the airport, she finally found a short article: "Crash Averted at Nassau International Airport."

The plane had nosedived, as she had seen, the result of a computer failure. At the last second, however, the pilot had been able to straighten the plane and complete a successful emergency landing. "Due to Captain Aballa's expertise, there were no injuries," the little story concluded.

"Thank God," Jayda mumbled as she texted Daphne the good news.

———

"I don't want these lenses," Jayda told the optometrist the following afternoon.

"Really?" Dr. Halstead said. "They're supposed to be much better quality. What don't you like about them?"

Jayda hesitated. "They're much too powerful. I see everything too clearly."

"I can lower the strength."

"That won't help. Just give me ordinary lenses, please...Can I ask you a question?"

"Of course."

"Has anyone else tried these new lenses?"

"No, not yet."

"Good. Please tell the manufacturer to discontinue them."

"Why?"

Jayda sighed. "As I said, they're much too strong. Here." She handed the silver-framed glasses to the optometrist. "I'll use my old glasses till you make me another pair."

Dr. Halstead watched as Jayda left the office. Then he picked up the phone and made a call. "The lenses work," he said to the voice at the other end. "Put them into production."

THE KEY

The small cardboard box was on the mat outside Ruben's apartment when he came home from work. Just his name—"RUBEN ALVAREZ"—had been printed in the center with a black marker.

Ruben picked up the box, which felt very light, almost empty. But it wasn't, because when he shook it, Ruben heard a muffled sound. He took the box inside, placed it on the kitchen table, and studied it.

Ruben knew the danger of opening an unknown package, having heard countless warnings about terrorist-planted bombs. But this little box was too light for a bomb—and Ruben didn't think anyone wanted to kill him.

Reaching into the drawer for a pair of scissors, he slit the tape and opened the box. After removing several crumpled sheets of newspaper, he pulled out the contents—one silver key. He checked the box again, looking for a note or instructions explaining what the key was for. But there was nothing.

Ruben twirled the key in his hand, contemplating what it could open. It wasn't shaped like an ordinary house key or even a car key. Instead, it looked old-fashioned—the kind of key you might use to crank up a music box or operate a game, only larger.

It had to open something. *But what? And why me?* Ruben wondered if his questions would be answered.

At work, Ruben couldn't stop thinking about the mysterious key. His job wasn't challenging—entering data for a medical group—so he had plenty of time to think. Since his thoughts usually involved incurable illnesses he might develop, the key was a welcome change.

A treasure chest? Ruben shook his head. That idea seemed too far-fetched. There had to be a better explanation. *An advertising scheme?* Then other people would have gotten keys too.

"Hey, Louise," he called to his coworker in the next cubicle. "Did someone leave a package on your doorstep yesterday?"

"No. Why're you asking?"

"Just curious. Thanks."

During the day, Ruben questioned several other employees about receiving boxes and no one else had.

The only person he could talk to about the key was Jesse— Ruben's best friend—actually his only friend. They met every Thursday night for dinner and drinks at Teddy's Bar & Grill on Allerton Avenue, but Jesse had cancelled two of the last three times.

"I've got a bad cough," was the first reason and then last week Jesse had backed out, saying, "I've got to meet someone."

The "meeting someone" excuse concerned Ruben. *Who was so important—more important than me?*

Tomorrow was Thursday and he'd insist Jesse join him at Teddy's. He needed his friend's take on the mysterious key.

"It does look different," Jesse agreed, examining the key as they sat at Teddy's bar, rather than in their usual booth. "Someone gave you this?"

Ruben nodded. "But I don't know who sent it or what the key's for."

"Forget about it then," Jesse said. "It must've been a mistake. Let's order our drinks because I've got to leave early tonight." He signaled the gum-chewing waitress, who ignored him and continued to wipe the counter.

"How about some burgers too?" Ruben asked.

Jesse shook his head. "Sorry, pal, but I've got someplace else to go tonight so I just have time for drinks."

"Where are you going?"

Instead of answering right away, Jesse studied the placemat and folded his hands. "I've been meaning to tell you..." he began and then stopped.

"Tell me what?"

"Okay." Jesse lifted his head and spoke quickly. "I met someone at work. She's divorced with a couple of kids and I've been seeing her."

"Oh."

"Is that all you have to say? How about, 'Congratulations on finding someone' or 'Good luck'?"

"Yeah, congratulations and good luck. I hope it works out for you."

"You don't sound real happy."

"Are you going to be seeing this woman on Thursday nights too?"

"Probably."

Ruben nodded. "At least I understand your situation now. Let's order the drinks so you'll be able to see your girlfriend."

———

Ruben had trouble falling asleep Thursday night. He kept thinking about Jesse and trying to feel happy for him, but it was hard. *What about me?*

Ruben knew he wasn't the best-looking guy, but he wasn't ugly either. Plenty of balding, slightly overweight men in their mid-forties had girlfriends, wives, and kids.

He understood part of the reason: his mother. He had lived at home with Mama and when he wanted to move out—that's when she got sick. *Ovarian cancer...*Ruben had stayed in the apartment, caring for her until her death three years ago.

Now it seemed like it was too late. Everyone else had leaped ahead of him, even Jesse.

Bianca. He did have his younger sister in New Jersey. But she had her own problems, having left Mario and raising two teenage girls, Yasmine and Celia, by herself. Ruben spoke to Bianca occasionally and visited her family for holidays.

"It's not enough," he muttered.

———

Ruben found the envelope on his doorstep Monday night. Again nothing was written outside except his full name in black upper-case letters. This time, however, Ruben hurried into the apartment, anxious to see what the envelope contained.

After ripping it open, he removed a single sheet of paper with one sentence written in the same black marker as his name: "OPEN THE LOCK WITH THE KEY AND YOU WILL BE SAVED."

Ruben placed the paper on the kitchen table and reread the words. *Open the lock? What lock? How?* "And what's this about me being saved," he said out loud. "Saved from what?"

Walking into the bedroom, Ruben took the oddly shaped key from his top dresser drawer and studied it. Then he set the key on the kitchen table next to the note.

For several minutes, he stared at the note and key until, shaking his head, he picked up both and put them in the dresser drawer.

———

Nothing else strange happened during the workweek so by the time Ruben arrived home Friday evening, he had stopped thinking about the mysterious key and note. But when he reached his apartment door, another letter with just his name printed on the envelope lay on the mat.

Ruben rushed inside to read the contents. Only two words were written in black upper-case letters on a small notepad page: "CAYUGA AVENUE."

Where's that? The street name didn't sound familiar. Grabbing his phone, Ruben typed the two words. There was a Cayuga Avenue in the north Bronx, near Van Cortlandt Park.

He stared at the phone for a moment, although he had already made up his mind. Tomorrow was Saturday, the start of another lonely weekend. Maybe this key and lock thing was dumb, but at least it was something different.

———

Because he didn't own a car, Ruben had to use public transportation to get to Cayuga Avenue. Saturday morning after breakfast, he took the subway to the Van Cortlandt Park station at Broadway and West 242nd Street, about a half-mile from his destination. Since the spring day was mild and sunny and Ruben loved to walk, the ten-minute stroll wasn't a problem.

When he reached Cayuga Avenue, Ruben glanced up at the green street sign and fingered the outside of his jacket pocket. The key was still there. Somewhere on this tree-lined residential street, he was supposed to find a lock his key would open.

Ruben walked along one side of the avenue, searching for an unusual lock. But it was a short street, with private homes and two apartment buildings, so his stroll took less than five minutes.

At the end of Cayuga Avenue, Ruben crossed the road and retraced his steps on the other side. The avenue was upscale—nicer than his—with mature trees and beautifully manicured shrubs flanking the apartment buildings. Nothing seemed unusual.

He repeated his walk, hoping other pedestrians wouldn't notice him. But the residents were involved with their own activities— mothers pushed toddlers in strollers, two teen boys laughed together—and no one looked at Ruben.

———

Towards the end of his second tour of Cayuga Avenue, Ruben spotted a building he'd missed earlier, probably because it was recessed behind several intertwined maple trees. The red brick structure was three stories high and didn't look like a home. *A school?* Ruben glanced up. There was no name on the building. In fact, it looked deserted.

Stepping through the trees, he reached the front door and eyed the lock. It was disappointingly ordinary, not a match for his odd-shaped key. Ruben gazed inside the uncovered window, but saw only a large empty room.

He rang the bell and waited. When no one answered, Ruben twisted the knob and the door opened. Entering the building, he again looked into the large room on his right. He had been correct. The room was empty.

Ruben turned to the closed door on his left and tried the knob. Although the door didn't open, it was another ordinary lock, not one his key would fit into.

Ignoring the stairway, he continued to the back of the building, passing another large room, again empty, and a small bathroom. Returning to the staircase, he hesitated for only a moment before climbing the steps.

———

Since the second floor contained just an unfurnished open space, Ruben climbed up the last flight of steps.

There were three rooms on the third floor—one to Ruben's left, another to his right, and a large empty room straight ahead. Both side doors were shut and when Ruben twisted the knobs, neither opened. But the locks were ordinary so he didn't attempt to use his key to open them.

Entering the vacant room, he stood in the center, hands on hips, wondering what to do next. That's when he noticed the closet in the left corner. He hadn't seen it immediately because the door was painted the same off-white shade as the room. Even the knob had been painted off-white. *The doorknob...*

Ruben rushed to the closet. The lock on the closet's doorknob had an unusual shape. He turned the knob, but once again the door was locked. Taking the key from his pocket, Ruben held it next to the lock and nodded his head.

———

Ruben stood in front of the locked door considering his options. He could simply walk away and forget about the strange key. *It's just a closet—a closet in an empty house.*

With the key raised in his right hand, Ruben took a step back. "OPEN THE LOCK WITH THE KEY AND YOU WILL BE SAVED," he remembered as he stared at the key and the lock. Then, before losing his nerve, Ruben inserted the oddly shaped silver key into the matching lock and opened the closet door.

Without stepping inside, Ruben stuck his head into the closet. It too was empty. However, as he shut the door, he heard a faint sound. He wasn't sure what the noise was, but it was coming from the closet.

Carefully, Ruben took one step and then another until he was fully inside.

———

Standing in the empty closet, Ruben still heard a noise in the right corner so he stuck his hand against that part of the wall and felt—nothing. Slowly, he again touched the wall and found he hadn't been mistaken. Although it looked solid, a section of the right side of the closet wasn't there.

Ruben put his right arm inside the opening and dangled it. When nothing happened, he did the same with his right leg and stared at himself in amazement. Only the left half of his body was visible. The right side was...*where?*

Taking a deep breath, Ruben pushed his head and the rest of his torso into the opening.

———

Ruben stood inside another empty closet. But in this closet, the noise was louder and he could tell what it was—music from a piano.

Leaving the closet, Ruben stepped into a large room that wasn't empty. It was filled with a pool table, ping-pong table, and various size couches. A massive bookcase covered one wall and a huge TV filled another.

Also, there was someone in the room. An elderly man sat on one of the couches reading a book.

"Excuse me," Ruben said to the man. "I'm really confused. Where am I?"

The man looked up from the book and smiled. "You're on the third floor of the Lillyfield Recreation Center," he said.

Ruben shook his head. "That's impossible. I was in an empty house on Cayuga Avenue, stepped through a closet, and ended up here. How can that be?"

"I never heard of Cayuga Avenue," the older man said, shrugging. "But now you're in Lillyfield and it's a darn good place to be. My name's Herb King." He stuck out his hand. "I'll be glad to show you around the center."

———

Herb and Ruben took the stairs down to the second floor, another large open room dominated by a white baby grand piano, where an African-American woman, wearing a pink suit and matching hat, played an unfamiliar melody. But Ruben recognized the sound. It was what he had heard inside the closet.

"Hey, Sally, this here's Ruben," Herb said to the lady in pink.

"Glad to meet you." Smiling, she lifted her long fingers from the piano and waved.

The two men descended the stairs to the first floor. "And this is the meeting place," Herb said as they stood in another large room filled with folding chairs. "That's about it."

Ruben was disappointed by the brief tour. Nothing in the rec center seemed unusual—except, of course, the way he had arrived there.

Ruben held out his arm to shake the older man's hand. "Thanks, again," he said, eying the front entrance. "I still don't understand what happened, but I'd like to look around outside now."

"Go ahead," Herb said, opening the door for Ruben. "It's a beautiful day. It's always a beautiful day in Lillyfield."

———

Ruben immediately realized he was no longer on Cayuga Avenue. This street was much wider, with no other houses except the recreation center. Everything else had been replaced by green space.

Sitting on a metal bench—which hadn't been there before either—Ruben considered the view. It was as if Van Cortlandt Park had swallowed Cayuga Avenue. That was impossible, but so was everything else.

The empty building was no longer empty, the street was completely different, yet here he was. Reaching into his jacket pocket,

Ruben removed the silver key and held it in front of his face.

"The key's amazing, isn't it?"

Ruben looked up at a woman smiling at him.

"You know about the key?" he said.

"I have one too." The attractive ponytailed woman, who seemed to be in her thirties, unzipped her shoulder bag and took out an identical key.

"What does all this mean?" Ruben asked.

"I'll be glad to tell you what I know," the woman said. "My name is Elena Cummings. Mind if I sit?"

"I'm Ruben Alvarez." He gestured towards the bench. "Please join me."

———

"The key came in an empty box, right?" Elena asked.

"Yes."

"And then you got a letter about using it in a lock."

"OPEN THE LOCK WITH THE KEY AND YOU WILL BE SAVED," Ruben recited.

"And then you got another letter with the name of a street."

"Cayuga Avenue."

Elena laughed. "My letter said Rosehill Drive."

Ruben stared at her. "You came here from a different street?"

"Yup, and probably a different city. I'm from Chicago."

"I'm from New York," he said, shaking his head. "How could that be?"

"Because this place isn't in our world. It's somewhere else. None of us knows exactly where we are—only that it's not part of anywhere on Earth." She looked at Ruben and smiled. "Does any of this make sense?"

"No."

Elena chuckled. "You're right. It doesn't make sense, but we're still here." She stopped smiling and studied Ruben. "Can I ask a personal question?"

"Go ahead."

"Were you happy before you got here?"

"No."

"That's why you were given the key. None of us liked our earlier lives."

Ruben looked at the woman. "Is it different here?"

She nodded. "Much different." Elena stood and held out her hand to Ruben. "Let me show you."

———

"All we know is that this place is called Lillyfield," Elena said as she and Ruben continued walking along the road that was no longer Cayuga Avenue. Ruben looked for a street name, but could find none. The road flowed into another unnamed street, this one lined with small cottage-like houses in numerous pastel colors—green, pink, yellow, pale blue.

Ruben realized he hadn't seen any cars on the roads and none of the little homes had garages. "Where are all the cars?" he asked.

"There are no cars here, no vehicles of any kind."

"No vehicles? Then how do you travel?"

Elena pointed to her feet. "You walk."

"But what if you want to go somewhere far away?"

"There is nothing far away. Everything is walking distance."

"What if it's bad weather?"

Elena shrugged. "There's no bad weather—no rain, no snow, no cold."

"I don't get it," Ruben said, shaking his head.

"None of us understands Lillyfield," Elena agreed.

———

To Ruben, the center of Lillyfield resembled an old-fashioned small town, a place from the middle of the twentieth century, like in old TV sit-com reruns. *Leave It to Beaver* and *The Andy Griffith Show* popped into his head.

He stood next to Elena on what could have been Main Street— although again there was no street sign—and scanned the line of shops. He saw a bakery, supermarket, and ice cream parlor, followed by toy, hardware, and clothing shops.

A few people drifted in and out of the stores. Elena waved to each of them and they all smiled at her.

"What kind of jobs do people have here?" Ruben asked.

"You do whatever work you want. You choose your job."

"Huh?" He looked at Elena.

"And you don't have to work if you don't want to."

"Then how do you earn money?"

Elena giggled. "We don't use money in Lillyfield. You just go into a store and take whatever you want or need."

Ruben pointed to a middle-age woman exiting the supermarket with a half-filled shopping cart. "You mean she took all that food?"

"Yup."

Ruben shook his head. "I don't understand."

"I know. But let's keep going. We have to find your new house."

———

Elena and Ruben left the retail section of town and entered another residential area, again filled with pastel cottages. "How do you know which is my house?" he asked.

"It'll be the last one. Every time someone new comes to Lillyfield, a house is added."

"By who?"

Elena shrugged. "We don't know. The house just pops up on the street."

Ruben stopped walking and stared at all the similar-looking cottages. "But without street names, how can you tell which house is which?"

"They all have numbers. This house is 36, see?" Elena pointed to two small blue numerals in the middle of the front door. Then, grabbing Ruben's hand, she gave it a small tug. "Come on. I think we'll find your house after the next two blocks."

———

They reached a street only half-filled with homes. "This must be the right place," Elena said, "because it's not finished yet." She ran down the block, stopping at the last house, a mint green cottage with the number 117 painted on the front door.

"Let's see if this is the one," she said. "Try your key."

Ruben inserted his key into the lock and the door opened.

"Welcome home, Ruben," Elena said.

The house was small, but comfortable. It was furnished in styles, colors, and patterns that matched Ruben's taste. "I would've picked out this couch in a store," he murmured, caressing the soft gray leather living room sofa.

"Whoever set up Lillyfield knows what each of us likes," Elena said. "I love everything about my house too."

Ruben sat in the gray couch and leaned his head back. "So what do I do now?"

"Whatever you want."

"I can just stay here and rest?"

"Sure."

"What if I want to do something?"

"As I said, you can get a job."

"How about entertainment?"

"There's no TV, radio, or computers, but we do have movies and music—any movie or song you want to see or hear."

"But I saw a TV in the recreation center."

"It's just a screen for playing DVDs."

"Phones?"

Elena shook her head.

"What about reading?"

"No newspapers or magazines, but you can find any book you want in the library."

Ruben smiled at Elena. "Maybe Lillyfield is heaven."

"Maybe it is," she said, returning his smile.

———

Ruben stood in the kitchen of his new house and gazed out the window. Even the view was something he had yearned for—trees and rolling hills—not apartment buildings.

After telling Ruben her house number—58—Elena had left, saying, "You've got a lot to think about."

He picked up the silver key that had taken him to Lillyfield and examined it. "Can everything really be this good here?" he whispered.

Leaving the key on the marble countertop, he walked to the refrigerator and opened it. Inside were Ruben's favorite foods—banana yogurt, sliced turkey breast—even his favorite bread, whole grain white. Realizing he was hungry, he prepared lunch. As expected, the turkey sandwich was delicious.

He took a short nap in his comfy new bed and woke up refreshed and curious. After changing into a pair of comfortable jeans and a gray tee shirt—clothing he would have chosen—he laced up a new pair of sneakers—a perfect fit—locked the door with his special key, and stepped outside to explore Lillyfield.

————

Residents were enjoying the early afternoon and everyone Ruben met either smiled or waved to him and he did the same. The people of Lillyfield were a mix of ages and nationalities. He passed women with babies; young children; teens; adults; older men and women, some with canes; and several couples his own age. There were white faces, black faces, brown faces—*like the United Nations...*

After Ruben walked through the small commercial section again, he headed to the recreational area, strolling a few miles along a flowery path until the trail ended abruptly at a stretch of woods.

Feeling adventurous, Ruben stepped into the narrow space between trees and continued walking. It was strangely quiet inside the forest and the lack of noise made Ruben realize he hadn't seen any animals or heard any birds since arriving in Lillyfield. Although the weather was still comfortably warm, he shivered and rubbed his arms.

Get out. The urge to leave the woods hit him suddenly with great force. Turning, Ruben tried to retrace his steps, but the trees all looked alike and he didn't recognize any landmarks.

Dummy! He tapped himself lightly on the head for his foolishness as he continued to search for a way out of the forest. When he reached a clearing he hadn't seen earlier, Ruben knew he was hopelessly lost, with no way to summon help. He sat on a broken log to think.

————

Which direction? Ruben no longer remembered where he'd come from. As he examined the ground leading into the open space, he noticed a section of trampled grass.

After re-entering the woods at that spot, he walked for at least a mile without seeing anything except more trees and not hearing any sounds except his footsteps and breathing, which was becoming heavier with each labored step.

Ruben dropped to his knees to rest. Several minutes later, he forced himself to continue, hoping he was making progress and not just walking in circles. Picking up a pointed branch, Ruben tried to etch a mark in a tree trunk, but the stick broke.

"What's the use?" he whispered, tossing the branch. Just then, Ruben saw a small beam of light and waded through the trees towards the yellow glint. As he got closer, he realized the light was flashing.

The forest ended and Ruben stood in an open field facing the light. It was a floodlight-type beam, stuck in the ground, pointing upward and flashing in a pattern—one blink, two blinks, one blink, three blinks, one blink...

Who was the signal for? Ruben looked into the sky and saw only clear blueness.

He sat on the grass next to the flashing light to rest and figure out what to do next. Staring at the forest, he shook his head. *Not there.* But this empty field seemed to stretch for many miles. Already exhausted from so much walking, Ruben knew if he continued in the same direction, he would be heading further from Lillyfield.

He listened for some sound—anything. However, as in the woods, there was only silence. Checking the sky again, he realized the sun was considerably lower so it had to be late afternoon. Not wanting to be alone in the open field in the dark, he walked away from the forest, hoping to find shelter beyond the field.

———

The empty field seemed endless and Ruben's legs ached. In addition to being tired, he was now thirsty. At least the temperature, even at twilight, was still comfortably warm.

He moved like an automaton, pushing his legs forward, determined to make it out of the spooky field before darkness. Finally, in the distance, Ruben saw lights, lots of them.

People! With a goal in sight, Ruben jogged towards the brightness, nearly tripping over his feet, even though the terrain was flat. When he reached the source of the lights, he dropped onto the ground, bewildered.

He was back in Lillyfield. The lights were from the stores in the shopping area. *How could that be?* After walking in the opposite direction, he'd returned to the place he had left.

————

Ruben needed to talk to someone about his perplexing discovery and the only person he knew how to find in Lillyfield was Elena. He trudged to the house numbered 58 and rang the bell.

"Ruben!" Elena exclaimed when she opened the door. "What a nice surprise! Come in."

He stumbled inside and collapsed on the living room couch.

"You look tired."

"Some water, please," Ruben whispered.

"Of course." She brought him a filled glass and Ruben downed it quickly.

"Thanks," he said.

"What happened to you?"

He recounted his strange experience. "What kind of a place is this?" he asked when he had finished. "It's like a big circle."

"Does it really matter?" she said. "You agreed that Lillyfield is nicer than where you came from."

"Yes, but..."

"Let's have dinner first. You must be hungry after all that walking."

"Sure, but..."

Elena interrupted Ruben again. "After we eat, we'll talk."

————

Elena broiled six lamb chops and baked two potatoes while Ruben prepared a salad. "How did you know this is my favorite meal?" he asked as he sliced a tomato.

"I didn't."

"Then it's a strange coincidence that you were planning to make this dinner."

"I wasn't."

Ruben looked at Elena, dumbfounded. "You just happened to have lamb chops, potatoes, and salad ingredients?"

"Yes, I found them in the refrigerator."

"You didn't know you had them?"

Elena nodded. "That's what's so great about this place. It knows what everyone likes."

"But that's impossible."

"Here's your impossible dinner," Elena said as she placed three lamb chops and a potato on his plate. "I'm sure the food will be excellent. It always is—and I'm not a great cook."

Ruben tasted a lamb chop and nodded at Elena. "This really is good."

———

"Now please tell me everything you know about Lillyfield," Ruben said to Elena after their meal. "Let's start with how long you've been here."

Elena shrugged her shoulders. "I don't really know."

"Why not? You can mark days off in a calendar."

"There are no calendars here."

"A newspaper would give you the date."

She shook her head. "No newspapers, remember?"

Ruben stared at her. "You can take a pencil and paper and write down each day's date."

"I tried doing that, but the numbers always disappeared. There are no clocks or watches here either. Ruben, they don't want us to know the time."

"Who are 'they'?"

"The ones who run Lillyfield—the ones who give us everything we want." She paused for a moment. "The same ones who gave you the key."

"People don't have the power to do all this." He waved at the room.

"I'm sure they're not people."

"Have you ever seen them?"

Elena shook her head again. "Nobody has."

"Are they invisible?"

"I don't know." She squirmed in her chair. "Can we talk about something else, please?"

"Okay," Ruben agreed. "When I left the forest, I saw a spotlight flashing signals to the sky. Have you ever heard about that light or seen it?"

"No."

Ruben studied Elena's face. She seemed to be telling the truth. "What else is here?" he asked.

Elena paused for a moment. "Nothing," she finally whispered.

"What?"

"There's nothing else, Ruben. Just this place."

He jumped up.

"Where are you going?"

"Back to the recreation center," he said, rushing to the door. "I'm getting out of here."

"You can't."

"What do you mean?"

"You can't go back."

Releasing the door, Ruben turned to face Elena. "I came through a closet."

She shook her head again. "The closet's gone. You won't find a way out."

"How do you know?"

"When I discovered I was trapped here, I tried leaving. Lots of people have tried." Walking slowly to Ruben's side, she took his hand. "I'm sorry, but this is your home now."

———

Ruben had attempted to be polite when he left Elena's house, but their talk greatly disturbed him. "Thanks for dinner," was all he'd mumbled.

Now he walked to the rec hall to check Elena's story. *The closet...*It had to be there.

The lights were on inside the building and Ruben raced up two flights of stairs to the third floor, seeing no one. Passing the pool table and ping-pong table, he ran to the back wall, looking for the closet door.

Nothing. He felt along the wall, hoping to find even a slight bulge that he could push through. But the entire wall was solid.

Thinking he might have been wrong about the door's location, Ruben sidled along the TV wall and then the bookcase wall, feeling for an opening. Again he found nothing.

Reaching inside his shirt pocket, Ruben took out the oddly shaped silver key. "I shouldn't have been so curious," he whispered, inserting the key inside one of the books on a middle shelf and purposely not looking at the title.

―――――

Without the key, Ruben no longer had access to his house, but he didn't care. He didn't want that custom-designed home—hadn't asked for it. *A place to sleep?* Although his legs ached, he wasn't tired after napping earlier in the day.

Ruben had borrowed a flashlight from Elena, telling her he might have difficulty locating his house at night. But he'd never intended to go there.

He needed the flashlight for another reason. *The spotlight...*Maybe that signal beam offered a clue to a way out. Turning on the flashlight, Ruben headed away from the houses, towards the darkness.

―――――

Although the stores were closed when Ruben reached the business section, most were dimly lit so he didn't need his flashlight until he reached the open field. Surrounded by total blackness, Ruben was surprised he wasn't more frightened. But his determination pushed him forward, despite the pains in his legs.

When he glimpsed the flashing beam, Ruben hurried his steps.

Panting heavily, he was about to run to the light when he heard something. He stopped and switched off his flashlight.

With no place to hide, Ruben dropped to the grass and listened to the sound—a two-way conversation in an unfamiliar language—strange bell-like tones, similar to musical notes.

Although he strained to see the speakers, Ruben couldn't get a good look. Since they would surely see him if he turned on his light, he remained flat on the ground and continued to listen.

The conversation got more animated, becoming more of a musical argument with loud screeching notes that made it less melodic. Then a third speaker entered the discussion, producing softer tones, like a peacemaker.

When the voices stopped, Ruben heard different noises—a series of mechanical squeaks, clangs, and thuds. The sounds seemed to drift overhead, getting lower until they faded. Glancing up, Ruben saw a triangular object floating high above. After a quick swoosh, the triangle zoomed ahead, disappearing into the blackness.

Ruben stayed still for several minutes. When he was certain he was alone, he walked to the flashing beam, which still aimed signals at the sky. Although he looked for the triangular object, he saw nothing.

———

In addition to being exhausted, Ruben was frustrated he hadn't found a way to return home. Instead, he'd discovered a new mystery. Who were those musical talkers who traveled in a triangle-shaped spaceship—and what did they look like?

As he walked towards Lillyfield's residential section, Ruben wanted to talk to Elena. But even though he had no idea of the exact time, he knew it was after midnight—too late for a visit.

Despite no longer having a key to his house, he planned to rest outside the cottage until morning. As Elena had promised, the temperature was still mild and the night clear.

Ruben again passed the dimly lit stores and continued to the streets filled with similar-looking pastel colored cottages. Most lights were off and no one was outside. He checked the house numbers until he found 117, his mint green cottage.

Ruben aimed the beam at his doorknob. "No!" he shouted, dropping the flashlight. Inserted in the lock was a key.

———

Sitting at his kitchen table, Ruben examined the key. It was the same odd-shaped silver key that had been left at his apartment door. Although he had been intrigued with it then, he wanted nothing to do with it now.

Trapped...But why had those strange-talking aliens—they had to be aliens—created this place? And what were they planning to do with the people here?

Ruben shook his head, too tired to think. Stumbling into the bedroom, he slipped under the sheets of his cozy new bed and instantly fell asleep.

———

When Ruben woke the next morning, his legs still ached, but his head felt clear. After a quick breakfast of cold cereal, he rushed out— not bothering to lock the door—and headed to Elena's house.

Ruben rang her bell and waited. But there was no answer.

Was she out? It seemed rather early, but she could have taken a morning walk. He sat on the doorstep, hoping Elena would return soon.

When she didn't appear, Ruben rang the doorbell of the house next door. No one answered. He walked up and down the block, ringing every doorbell and getting no response.

Finally, Ruben tried opening each front door, but the doors were all locked and there were no keys in any of them.

Ruben turned and ran from Elena's block.

———

The stores weren't yet open so Ruben knew it still had to be early. He nodded at two joggers, glad some people remained in Lillyfield, and slogged through the open field, ignoring the pain in his sore legs.

When he saw the beam flashing in the distance and hurried towards it, he noticed people—lots of them. Ruben fell to the grass and watched.

A large triangular spaceship rested on the ground, its door open. A line of perhaps thirty people—men, women, and children in various states of dress, a few even naked—faced the door and, one by one, entered the ship, all unwillingly, some kind of force propelling them forward. Although their mouths were open, the moving people uttered no sounds.

He recognized Herb King—the older man in the rec center—as he was swept inside. And then...*Elena!* She was the last person in line, crying silently as she drifted closer to the ship.

The musical notes. Ruben heard them again. Straining his eyes, he searched for the source of the sounds and saw two aliens, tall slender beings, standing by the door and monitoring the people as they tumbled into the spaceship. He hadn't noticed the pair before because they were so pale, nearly translucent.

Ruben crawled towards Elena, hoping the preoccupied aliens didn't see him. Grabbing her right pajama leg, he pulled as hard as he could, but she continued to slide forward.

Elena glanced down. "Ruben?" she mouthed.

The line was now much shorter with maybe ten people in front of her. "Try to fall," Ruben whispered. Grasping both of her ankles, he tugged again. There was a slight ripping sound and Elena dropped to the ground.

"Crawl fast," Ruben ordered as he scurried from the ship. Turning his head, he was relieved to see Elena following.

———

When he felt they were far enough away, Ruben stopped crawling and stood. Elena did the same. "To the stores," he said, pointing to Lillyfield's shops in the distance.

They walked silently, Elena barefoot, until they reached the shopping area. Pointing to her striped pajamas and shoeless feet, she said, "I have to change my clothes and get shoes."

"You can't go back to your house."

"The clothing store has shoes too. I'll only need a few minutes."

"Is there a coffee shop?"

"The Bread Basket's on the next block."

"Meet me there."

———

As they sat at a small round table eating croissants and drinking coffee, Elena, now dressed in jeans and a black tee shirt, looked at Ruben. "Thank you," she whispered.

Ruben nodded. "I want to hear everything that happened this morning."

Lowering the pastry, Elena sighed. "I was sleeping until something lifted me out of bed and carried me out of the house, all the way to that place with the spaceship and those creatures, and I couldn't do anything to stop it. I tried screaming at first, but no words came out of my mouth.

"I saw the other people from my street—Linda Fuller, her husband, and little boy; Mr. Gambini, my next-door neighbor; and everyone else. We looked at each other, but none of us could move." Tears fell from her eyes and she wiped them away. "Then everyone was sucked into that ship."

Ruben took a sip of coffee. "Do you still have your key?"

"Why are you asking?"

"I think that's what's keeping us here—our keys. I stuck mine inside a library book in the rec building, but when I returned to my house, the key was in the lock."

Elena reached into her pants pocket and took out her key. "I was in bed wearing pajamas so I didn't take this with me. I'm sure of it. And I certainly didn't put it in these new jeans."

"If I'm right and they're using the keys to control us, we have to find a way to get rid of them."

"How? You said yours came back too."

Ruben shrugged. "I don't know yet, but unless we find an answer, we'll end up on that spaceship like the people on your block."

"What do you think will happen to my neighbors?" Elena whispered.

"Nothing good."

"So what do we do now?" Elena asked, lowering her cup.

Ruben took a sip of coffee before speaking. "Did you ever hear talk about aliens or spaceships?" he finally asked.

"No," Elena said. "I'm sure nobody knows."

"Then we have to tell them."

"They won't believe us."

"You're right. We need proof."

———

"Where are we going?" Elena asked as she hurried to keep up with Ruben.

"To your block. I want to see what's there now."

"You know what's there. You said the houses were all empty."

"Let's check anyway," Ruben said. He stopped at one of the residential intersections. "Which is your block?"

Elena pointed to the left. "Mine is the street after this, with house numbers starting at forty-six."

When she and Ruben reached the spot Elena had indicated, they found only an empty grass-covered field. Elena sank to the ground, tears streaming down her face. "Where are all the houses?" she whispered. "It's like none of us ever lived here."

"Give me your key," Ruben said.

Elena took the key from her pocket and handed it to him. "What are you going to do with it?"

"Maybe if we drop the key where your house used to be, they'll think it fell out when they took you to the ship." He shrugged. "It's worth a try...Where do you think your house was?"

———

"We have to convince everyone in Lillyfield to get rid of their keys," Ruben told Elena as they walked back to the stores.

"They won't do it."

"We have to try."

"How?"

"Post warnings everywhere. Write something like, 'Stay out of your house! The people in houses forty-six through...'"

He turned to Elena.

"Sixty-two."

"...were taken away in an alien spaceship!'"

Elena shook her head. "The signs will disappear immediately. Remember, nothing you write lasts."

"Then we have to talk to them—maybe get everyone in the big room in the rec center, explain what happened to you, and mention the names of the missing people."

"No, Ruben. They won't believe us and they'll think of an excuse why those people are gone. Even though they're trapped, most everyone loves being in Lillyfield. I've heard them call this place Paradise or Eden." She looked at Ruben and shrugged. "We need real proof."

"The empty block?"

"How long do you think that land will be vacant? New houses pop up all the time."

"The aliens," Ruben murmured. "We have to show them the aliens."

"And the ship," Elena added.

———

"Wouldn't it be better to kill the aliens?" Elena asked Ruben as they sat on a bench near the stores.

"How? They're so powerful." Ruben waved his hands. "They created all this—and even if we managed to destroy them, I'm sure we'd die too."

"Then how do we show people the aliens without being forced into their ship?"

"We watch the beam, see when the spaceship returns, and find out if there's some kind of schedule."

"For taking more people away?"

Ruben nodded.

"You want to stay outside, on the grass near the flashing light, and wait?"

"Yes."

Elena felt each pocket of her jeans. "Well, here's some good news," she said, smiling. "My key didn't come back."

"Maybe my idea worked," Ruben said.

Ruben and Elena lay side by side on the grass, watching the flashing beam. Ruben knew it was transmitting a signal, using a series of short and long flashes—some kind of code—so he tried to discern a pattern, a difficult task without paper and pencil.

They had been there for about an hour when Ruben turned to Elena. "I think I've got it," he said. "The series goes about two minutes, ends with a long flash, and starts again with three short flashes...Now." He pointed to the light.

Elena watched and then nodded. "Yes, I can see it too." She looked at Ruben with widened eyes. "But I never would have figured that out. You're really smart."

Ruben felt his face getting warm, but didn't speak. Instead, he continued to stare at the beam, concentrating on memorizing the pattern.

They lay on the ground for many hours. At some point, Elena fell asleep and Ruben listened to her soft snores as he continued to monitor the beam. Not long after sunset, when the sky was nearly black, he noticed a change in the flashes.

"Elena," he whispered, shaking her gently. "Wake up. Something's happening."

———

Elena again stared at the beam with Ruben. "It's doing the same short flashes, over and over," she said. "Even I can see the difference."

Ruben pointed to the darkened sky. "Look," he whispered.

The triangular spaceship hovered above them, perhaps fifty feet high.

"Crawl backwards," Ruben said softly. "We can't let them see us."

"Unless they already have," Elena murmured as she followed Ruben away from the beaming light.

When they could no longer see the flashing beam or the spaceship, Ruben stood. "I think we're okay now," he said. "Let's get back to Lillyfield."

"And?"

"And take people to see the ship."

"But that's dangerous."

"Of course it's dangerous," Ruben agreed. "But we have to prove that the aliens exist."

———

"There's a spaceship with aliens in Lillyfield," Ruben told the mustached man who answered the doorbell. "And the aliens are taking people away in it."

"You're crazy!" the man said, slamming the door.

Ruben remained at the doorstep, stunned by the response. "What did I do wrong?" he asked Elena.

"Nothing, but you do sound crazy."

"Maybe if you talk, they'll listen."

She shook her head. "I'll just sound like a loony lady."

"What if I tell them there's some other kind of danger here?"

"Like what?"

"An earthquake or an attack?"

"They still won't believe you." Elena grabbed Ruben's arm, pulling him away from the door. "I've been in Lillyfield longer than you and most people are so happy to be here that they won't listen to anything you say. They'll just stay until the aliens come..." Her voice faded.

"Even when they discover their neighbors are missing?"

"They'll pretend nothing's happened."

Ruben shook his head. "I have to try more houses. Maybe someone will listen."

He and Elena rang the doorbells of every cottage on the street. Most people answered the bell, but no one listened to either Ruben or Elena—and nearly every resident slammed the door in their faces.

One elderly woman smiled and wagged her finger at Ruben. "Are you trying to be funny?" she asked.

"This is no joke, ma'am," he said.

"Well, I'm not going anywhere," she said. "Lillyfield is the best thing that ever happened to me. Good night."

She was one of the few who didn't slam the door.

———

"What now?" Elena asked as she hurried to keep up with Ruben.

"I'll write a warning note and leave it in the rec center."

"The note will disappear."

"What if I etch the words in the ground?"

"You can try, but I'm sure it won't work either."

After finding a pointy stick behind the path, Ruben aimed his flashlight on the ground and wrote: "ALIENS WITH A SPACE SHIP ARE TAKING PEOPLE AWAY!"

As soon as he dotted the exclamation point and stepped back, the indentations in the grass filled in so that his words were no longer visible.

"I told you...Oh no!"

Although Ruben couldn't see the expression on Elena's face in the darkness, he heard the despair in her voice. "What's wrong?" he asked.

"This," she replied, shoving her key in front of his face.

————

"Follow me," Ruben ordered, changing direction.

"Where to?"

"The ship, if it's still there."

Ruben walked so quickly that twice Elena had to ask him to slow down. When they saw the flashing beam in the distance, both dropped onto the grass.

"I see the ship," Elena whispered. "What should we do?"

"We have to toss our keys inside."

"How can we get close enough to do that without the aliens seeing us?"

"I don't know, but it's our only chance," Ruben said softly.

As they crawled side by side in the darkness towards the triangular ship, Ruben tapped Elena's shoulder and pointed ahead.

She glanced in the direction of his arm. One pale alien, his translucent body almost invisible against the night sky, stood next to the open door of the ship.

Ruben urged Elena forward until they were less than twenty feet from the alien and the spaceship. Then he took his key from his pocket and held out his hand.

As Elena extended her arm to give Ruben her key, she froze.

"What's wrong?" he whispered.

Still clutching the key, Elena bounced up and like the previous night, began gliding to the ship.

"No!" Ruben screamed. Standing, he dropped the flashlight and using both hands, wrenched the key from her fingers while she continued to drift to the door of the ship.

Hearing the noise, the alien sentry took several steps toward Ruben and thrust out a long, slender arm. Ruben ducked under the alien's limb and as Elena floated to the ship's entrance, flung both keys inside.

———

Blackness...total blackness.

Ruben no longer saw Elena, the ship, the alien, or the night sky. He still stood in the dark, but his feet were on a floor inside a building. Sticking out his hand, he felt a wall. Moving carefully, he followed the short wall around the corners until he realized he was again in an empty closet. When he turned the knob, he was relieved the door wasn't locked.

The room he stepped into was dark, but not as black as the closet because, through the curtainless windows, an outside streetlamp provided a smidgen of light.

Ruben knew he wasn't in the Lillyfield Recreation Center because this room was completely unfurnished—no pool table, bookcase, or TV.

Without the aid of a flashlight, he walked carefully down two flights of stairs and out of the house. Ruben immediately recognized the street. It was Cayuga Avenue.

Elena? "She's somewhere in the real world too," he murmured. *Elena Cummings from Chicago.* "I'll find her."

www.ingramcontent.com/pod-product-compliance
Lightning Source LLC
Chambersburg PA
CBHW060930180626
46817CB00004B/1478